Ginger was too fresh-faced and innocent, Zach thought.

Yet she hadn't asked about his arm. Or his dream. Did she know?

Ginger sat at the end of the couch and tucked her bare feet under his blankets. "I'm surprised you don't have a family of your own."

An interesting way of asking why he wasn't married. "Never got around to it, I guess."

"How come?"

He gave her the truth. "I saw too many guys torn up over leaving their wives and kids. Having to shut down to do the job. I didn't want that. What about you? No boyfriends?"

She looked away. "Ah, no."

"How come?" He repeated her words.

She shrugged. "They're a hassle."

Her fingers brushed his bare skin near the scar and she froze. "When did you get this?"

That raw whisper made him look into her wide brown eyes. "Three years ago."

She looked horrified. Her hair tickled his shoulder and he inhaled quick and sharp. She smelled nice. Really nice. Like flowers and rain. He caught her wide eyes.

Did she feel it, too, this hum of awareness between them?

Jenna Mindel lives in northwest Michigan with her husband and their three dogs. A 2006 Romance Writers of America RITA® Award finalist, Jenna has answered her heart's call to write inspirational romances set near the Great Lakes.

Books by Jenna Mindel

Love Inspired

Maple Springs

Falling for the Mom-to-Be
A Soldier's Valentine

Mending Fences
Season of Dreams
Courting Hope
Season of Redemption
The Deputy's New Family
His Montana Homecoming

A Soldier's Valentine

Jenna Mindel

LOVE INSPIRED BOOKS

ISBN-13: 978-0-373-81891-4

A Soldier's Valentine

This edition published by arrangement with Love Inspired Books.

www.Harlequin.com

Printed in U.S.A.

Finally, brothers and sisters, whatever is true, whatever is noble, whatever is right, whatever is pure, whatever is lovely, whatever is admirable—if anything is excellent or praiseworthy—think about such things. Whatever you have learned or received or heard from me, or seen in me—put it into practice. And the God of peace will be with you.

—*Philippians* 4:8–9

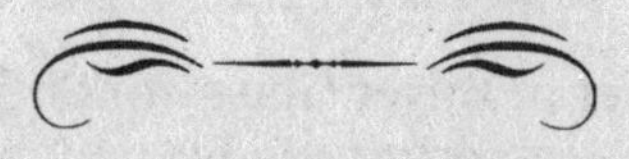

To those who serve.

Acknowledgments

Lawrence Fry, SFC, US Army, Retired. Thank you for your amazing insight into rank and structure, as well as answering my many questions about the army. Hopefully, I got it right.

Harry Boyer of Boyer Glassworks. Thank you for sharing your knowledge and taking the time to give a glass demonstration that really brought this incredible art to life.

Chapter One

There was nothing quite like a small-town parade welcoming home one of their own from active duty to inspire pride. Ginger Carleton breathed in the cold January air, feeling very proud that Maple Springs had embraced her idea. The short parade had gone off without a hitch, and even the mayor had been pleased.

Getting folks downtown in winter was always a challenge, but then Zach Zelinsky's return made for the perfect opportunity. One she wasn't about to let go.

There he was!

Ginger's heart beat a little faster. Captain Zach was her new landlord, and he walked toward her with purpose. They hadn't met in person despite the fact that the man had not only bought *her* building where she lived and operated a small tea shop, but he'd raised her rent, too. He'd informed her of that along with his plan to open a glassblowing studio next door in one professional, but very impersonal, letter.

She thought glass an odd choice for over six feet of hardened brawn standing like a statue before her in his military uniform. Atop his broad shoulders were two silver bars, and his chest was a patchwork of official-looking pins and patches.

Captain Zachary Zelinsky made for an impressive sight.

And scary.

Surely, he'd intimated an enemy or two with that deep scowl. A look that might make a lesser man run, but Ginger dug in her heels and held her position. He'd searched *her* out and she wasn't going anywhere. She might even tell him what she thought of his letter.

She heard the snaps of American flags that had been posted along Main Street as they whipped in the bitter wind. No snow fell today in northern Michigan. No sunshine, either. Gray clouds rippled in a gray sky above. The Maple Springs high school band had long since stopped playing patriotic marches, and her surroundings faded into the expanse of dark winter coats dotted by colorful hats and scarves and kids.

She focused on the army captain in front

of her. Not hard to do. Zach Zelinsky loomed larger than life.

Ginger pulled off her fuzzy mitten and extended her hand. She exhaled a long plume of cold breath, but it didn't eliminate the feeling of free-falling. "Nice to finally meet you, Captain Zach."

He took her hand with his warm, calloused fingers and squeezed. Firm and sure. His icy blue eyes were cold as Lake Michigan. Zach Zelinsky's letter of introduction spelling out her new lease terms had been equally frosty.

She swallowed hard. Okay, maybe she wouldn't mention his letter. Maybe never.

"Ms. Carleton." The tone of his voice rang deep. The quiet kind of sound that masked deadly strength. "I understand I have you to thank for this nonsense."

"And a bang-up job, don't you think?" With knees nearly knocking, Ginger gave him her best curmudgeon-taming smile. Playing nice was always better. God had taught her that through the scriptures.

Then the truth kicked in and made her squirm.

Okay, maybe she hadn't really played nice. She knew Captain Zach wouldn't be pleased by a parade, but he didn't have to growl about it. Helen Zelinsky had warned that her oldest son didn't want a fuss, but that was too bad. Maple Springs wanted to honor one of its own, and a parade brought folks downtown during a slow time of year. And she was one of the many shop owners who needed the foot traffic.

A glimmer of amusement barely lifted one side of his mouth. "If you say so."

What would he look like if he truly smiled?

That image made her pulse skitter, and Ginger pulled her hand back. He was her landlord now, and their handshake should have long since ended. "Did you really think you could sneak home unnoticed?"

"I suppose not." He stood straighter, if that was possible. His eyes remained cool, but not as cold as before.

She noticed the deep lines etched in the corners of those eyes. No doubt from squinting rather than laughter. Captain Zelinsky was killer handsome but looked like a man who needed a good laugh. And he wasn't exactly a young man, either.

Annie, her best friend and soon to be Captain Zach's sister-in-law, had said he was in his late thirties. The traces of gray in his short brown hair made him look older, though. Deep scowl aside, he still looked amazing. Amazing enough to make her breath catch.

And she needed to stop staring. "I received your letter. When will you open your shop?"

"As soon as the furnaces are inspected."

Ginger nodded. State requirements had to be met. And Sally, the previous owner, had told her that Zach had purchased her old ceramic kiln. For what, Ginger wasn't sure. Did glass get baked like ceramics? She wished she knew, but every time Ginger had stopped next door to introduce herself, Captain Zach hadn't been around. And maybe that had been a good thing. She got the feeling that she should let her irritation go when it came to his letter. Not much she could do about it anyway, now that the building was his.

At least the sounds of pounding and soldering and the whir of metal saws and drills might finally stop. Glassblowing wasn't a noisy business, but setting up for it sure was. She looked forward to the return of quiet.

The mayor suddenly swooped between them. "Come, Captain, there's someone you should meet."

"Yes, sir." Zach didn't move. Instead, he looked right through her. "I'll see you soon."

"Yep." Ginger flushed. She had to admit she looked forward to that despite the dollop of agitation that went with finding Captain Zach attractive.

Military men were not her thing. Growing up with a father who'd barked orders like a drill sergeant made her steer clear of authoritative types. Especially grumpy ones. But then, she steered clear of most men, preferring to keep her heart safe.

She watched the tall army captain walk away with his back ramrod straight and his footsteps slow but steady. He looked like a man who didn't dole out his approval easily. The man didn't hurry, either. And he sure didn't look in the mood to meet people. He better get over that real quick. People in Maple Springs loved to check out new businesses, and his glass studio was bound to be a target for the curious shoppers.

Speaking of shoppers, she had tea to sell. And she'd better sell a lot of it today, because her bank account was looking pretty wan. The price of tea was up, and her customers were down. And with that increase in rent…

She clenched her jaw. Not a good start to her year.

Making her way through the crowd that lingered, Ginger headed for her shop that sat on the corner of Main and Bay Streets. She spotted Lewis Brown coming toward her up ahead and quickly crossed the street. Annie called him the "book-man" because he worked at the library.

But Ginger called him a nuisance. He'd asked her out twice, and both times she'd turned him down. One of these days she'd have to tell him straight up that she wasn't interested, but not today.

Confrontation wasn't something she relished on a good day. And today wasn't exactly a good day. Not yet, anyway. Not until she had some sales.

Hurrying to get back to her shop, she glanced at the other stores along Main filling up with shoppers. Christmas decorations still teased from inside storefront windows even though it was the middle of January. Greenery-stuffed window boxes and velvet-bowed wreaths hung from doors.

It still looked like Christmas in Maple Springs and would remain so until the weather warmed. Few decorations were taken down earlier than the end of March with the exception of the Center Park Christmas tree. That had been cleared away last week.

The cold air made her hasten her steps. Slipping on a patch of ice, she bobbled but caught herself and stayed upright. A strong hand gripped her shoulder, steadying her. Fearing it might be Lewis, she looked up and breathed easy when it wasn't.

"Thanks."

Matthew Zelinsky chuckled and let go. "I don't know how you walk in those things."

Ginger laughed, too, glancing at her high-heeled-boot indulgence. "It takes skill." Then she looked around. "Where's Annie?"

"Home with the baby. She didn't want to take John out in this cold."

Ginger smiled. "She's hogging that little guy all to herself."

"She loves being a mom," Matthew said.

"Tell me something I don't know." At thirty-two, Ginger's biological clock had a few ticks left, but then she wasn't exactly looking for a husband. She hadn't met any she considered worth the trouble. Or the risk.

Matthew was one of the good ones. He had stepped in to help after Annie's husband had died, and they'd ended up falling in love. As first mate on a Great Lakes freighter, Matthew was home until late March when the shipping season started up again. "By the way, my mom's having a get-together in two weeks, and we'd like you to come."

"A prenuptial celebration? Sure, I'm in." Ginger was thrilled that Matthew had given Annie an engagement ring at New Year's. They planned a small, informal wedding the week before Valentine's Day.

"More of a welcome home for Zach."

"Oh…" She'd agreed too soon.

"I'll tell Annie that you're going. She'll be glad to have you there. I think my family overwhelms her at times. See ya." Matthew waved as he trotted off.

Ginger waved back. She knew how Annie felt. Captain Zelinsky had certainly overwhelmed *her*. And he hadn't been happy about a welcome-home parade. Not one bit. How would he take a welcome-home party with his huge family?

Zach woke with a start. His fists were full of sheet and bedspread and his T-shirt stuck to his back. He looked at the clock blaring red numbers that read 5:15 a.m., and swung his legs over the side of the bed. With his elbows resting on flannel-covered knees, he forced the shaking to stop by breathing deep.

A soft knock followed by the creak of the door confirmed that he woke someone else up with his thrashing. "Zach?"

"I'm okay, Mom. Go back to bed." He hoped she'd leave but knew otherwise. She was his mom. She'd try to make things all better like always, but he didn't have a skinned knee. This couldn't be healed with a kiss and a cartoon-covered bandage.

She entered the dark room and sat next to him. "How often?"

"What?"

"Do you dream like this?" She spoke softly, not calling them by name.

He didn't blame her. He didn't call them by name either, but he'd definitely had the same nightmare over and over since coming home. Today's parade, his uniform and the flags must have triggered what he'd tried to bury. But the horror of seeing his men torn to pieces in an ambush wouldn't stay buried. He'd been helpless then, and he was helpless now.

He'd led them there.

Zach let out the breath he'd been holding. "I don't know. Often enough, I guess."

"Oh, honey." His mom put her hands on his shoulders and kneaded the tight muscles there. She also mumbled under her breath.

Leaning closer, he realized his mom prayed. For him.

He closed his eyes, too. *Jesus, please…*

He'd taken his Lord's name in vain way too many times in his life. He'd also said the name in repentance and as a prayer. Now, he begged. For what, he still couldn't put to words. Peace eluded even though he was out of the service. Even though he'd talked to a counselor at the VA. Even though the mayor had introduced him to the director of the local VA office here. Would it help to keep talking? Zach didn't think so.

Buying a building where he could make things with glass might bring him the peace he sought. It's what he'd planned for after he retired. He just hadn't figured he'd have to retire this soon.

God knew he wanted to forget. But some things a person never forgot, including the notification letter that he'd been part of the army's reduction in force initiative. He'd received a letter during his last deployment that his service was no longer needed.

He stood and kissed the top of his mother's head. "Thanks, Mom. Now go back to bed."

She searched his eyes. "You're not going to sleep, are you?"

"No." He didn't want to repeat that *dream*. "Don't tell Dad."

His mom's eyes narrowed. "He'd be the right person to talk to. He could introduce you to a friend at the VA office here. They have a program—"

"No." Zach cut her off. He'd had enough talking on base. Seeing the hurt look in his mom's eyes, he softened. "I already met the guy, but not now. Not yet."

She didn't approve, he could plainly see that,

but she nodded anyway. Zach's mother never went back on her word. She'd protected him as a kid. His father hadn't known about the middle school brawls Zach had been in until many years later.

"I'm going to the shop to get some work done." He needed to get settled into his own place where he wouldn't wake his parents with his dreams. He needed to do something to keep his mind engaged in other realities. He needed to leave.

His mom gave him a worried look. "Be careful, honey. It's dark out there."

"I will." He chuckled.

He knew all about darkness. He'd faced far worse than the winding ten-mile drive into Maple Springs. By the time he'd thrown on clothes, made a thermos filled with coffee and climbed into his Jeep, Zach looked forward to going into town.

He wanted quiet but not isolation. He'd never been a fan of big crowds, so city life was out. But living atop his own glass studio in a small town that shriveled up to nothing during the winter months was exactly what he'd had in mind when the time came. And that time was now.

His parents had offered him land to build on, but now more than ever he needed busywork.

Distraction from his thoughts. A vision of that perky redhead named Ginger flashed through his mind. She looked too young for him. And cheerful in a cheeky sort of way that intrigued as much as irritated him. She probably hadn't experienced an unpleasant day in her short life.

It didn't take long before he pulled into the narrow back alley that ran the length of one block of Main. Streetlights above gave him plenty of light to see the back entrances of several buildings that were on each side. Each one had its own stout driveway, and he pulled next to a cherry red Volkswagen Beetle with a ladybug decal on its trunk. Right below that was a Love Michigan bumper sticker in the shape of a heart. Hometown pride. Or rather, home state.

The car had to be Ginger's. She rented not only her shop but the larger apartment of the two above, on the second floor.

The woman he'd purchased the building from had tried to make the long-term lease with Ms. Carleton and her tea shop a condition of the purchase. Zach had negotiated those terms down to a year at a time with the promise that he wouldn't simply kick Ginger to the curb without proper notice.

Zach had no intention of taking over the whole building just yet. Not until he grew his business. Having a stable rental income right off the bat appealed, but he couldn't have kept the ridiculously low rent. He'd had to raise it to help cover his loan payment.

He got out of his Jeep and looked at the car. The VW fit his vibrant tenant with the flaming hair and soft freckles. He heard the back door open, and Ginger stepped outside dressed for a jog. Her reflective striped clothes announced a serious runner.

"Morning," he said.

Startled, she grasped her neck, which was draped with a pink fleece scarf. "You scared the living daylights out of me!"

He chuckled.

She wasn't nearly as tall as he remembered from the parade, but she wasn't short, either. In fact, Ms. Carleton was perfectly sized.

Snow fell softly in the still morning darkness, wetting his face. He realized that he stood in her path and turned sideways, giving her room to pass.

She flashed him a nervous-looking smile and walked closer, then slipped on the ice.

He reacted fast.

Her arm slammed against his, knocking the thermos of coffee out of his hand. It hit the cement with a metallic clink. Zach managed to grab her waist and pulled her close.

"Oof." She landed hard against his chest and looked up. "Oh!"

As if receiving a blow to his head, he lost his bearings staring into her big brown eyes. She made a really nice armful. But before he could shift, or even wrap his other arm around her, she scrambled out of his grasp.

"Sorry." With cheeks blazing, Ginger wouldn't look at him. Instead, she searched the ground.

He'd forgotten about his thermos but found the silver tube resting against his tire and went for it. She did, too, and they bumped heads.

Rubbing her forehead, she giggled. The nervous, girlish sound slapped his ears, reminding him that she was too young. "I'm so sorry."

"No problem." He stood, empty-handed. This immediate attraction that flared in him might be a problem. Big problem.

"I hope it's not glass inside."

"What?" He couldn't form another word. Ms. Carleton had a way of tying up his tongue.

"Your thermos. If the center is glass, it's likely broken."

He bent and retrieved his mother's container and shook it. It rattled like a rice-filled salt shaker. There went his morning coffee. He looked around. "Is there any place I can get a cup of coffee this early?"

"Not this time of year." She looked thoughtful a moment and then smiled. She had a beautiful smile. Warm and sunny. "I make a mean cup of spiced chai if you like tea."

"I don't."

She shrugged. "The least I can do is fix you a cup of coffee then. I have a single-serving machine inside and there might be some coffee packs left over from my Christmas help if you're interested."

"Yeah, sure." He followed her and tossed the broken thermos in the outside trash bin.

She pulled a small bundle of keys from the zippered pocket of her fleece jacket and unlocked the back door. There was one entrance into a small foyer with two doors leading to their respective shops and a flight of stairs up to their apartments above. She flicked on the lights and stepped into the back room of her shop. "In here."

The first thing that hit Zach was the pleasant scent of cinnamon and something more subtle but sweet. He scanned the relatively bare shelves with rolls of Christmas-colored wrapping paper and bows and wicker baskets. There was a small table with a couple of chairs shoved against a wall opposite a microwave, half fridge and counter with sink. Magazines littered that table.

"Your break room?" he asked.

"And lunch room and basket-making room and office. You name it, this is it. I have a college girl who works for me during the summer months and over Christmas break. She drinks coffee, so there might still be some in here." She dug into a wire basket of little plastic containers and lined up three, side by side. "Take your pick, mocha or hazelnut flavored and plain."

"Plain."

He watched while Ginger inserted the container of coffee into the machine. Then she slipped a mug under the spout. She didn't wear a trace of makeup that he could tell. And she looked about college aged, even though he knew she couldn't be *that* young. Maybe midtwenties.

Still, a baby compared with his thirty-eight years.

"It'll take a few minutes to warm up." She leaned against the counter. "Cream or sugar?"

"Just black."

They fell silent while the coffee machine revved and beeped.

He nodded toward her store. "Mind if I take a look?"

"Go ahead. The light's on the right-side wall."

He was already in motion and gave a cursory glance at the racks of spices and huge glass jars of what looked like dried-up twigs and leaves. Decorative tins and teapots lined one wall. The Spice of Life was a nice play on words. Cute. Like the owner.

"Many of those teapots were made by Sally, the woman who used to own this building." Ginger stood next to him and offered a cup of steaming, strong-smelling coffee.

He accepted the mug with a nod and took a deep sip. "I never met Sally. I dealt with her Realtor for the most part."

"She's a super nice old lady. Our shops connect through that sliding glass door." She pointed at their shared wall that was mostly glass. "Sally and I left it open during business hours. Comes in handy watching each other's store, and we shared many of the same customers."

"Hmm." Probably a good idea to continue. Especially since he was going it alone until he knew what kind of income he might expect.

"Well, sorry to push you out, but I really need to get my run in before a chamber staff meeting later this morning. You can return the mug later."

He held up his coffee. "Thanks."

"Sure. We have an open chamber meeting later this week. You should attend, meet the other merchants and see how we can help support your business in this community."

"I'll think about it." He wasn't much for local politics, nor was he good at mingling.

She gave him a smile that nearly knocked him over. "There's really good food. The fancy dinner club around the corner is sponsoring it this month. You won't be sorry."

Did she realize the power she wielded with a simple look? "Maybe."

"I'll hold you to that."

"Uh, yeah." He made his escape before he said something stupid.

Ginger Carleton was cheerful with tart-sweetness rolled into one attractive package. Not that he'd ask her out. Dating his tenant would be completely inappropriate, like dating a woman under his command. And he was tired of seeing people under his command damaged—or worse. Not to mention that she was too young for him and better kept off-limits. Way off-limits.

"Well, Ginger, what do you think? Can you get the merchants on board?" Brady Wilson, the chamber president, waited for her response.

Ginger leaned back in her chair. The scowling face of Captain Zach came to mind, but she pushed that image aside. As liaison between the merchants and the chamber, it was her job to rally the troops, so to speak. "I don't know. I mean, other than the slight chance of our town being highlighted in the statewide tourism campaign, what's in it for them?"

Or her, for that matter.

Decorating specifically for Valentine's Day was an expense she hadn't planned for. She had a few things, everyone did, but a big storefront display contest meant going all out. Something everyone did at Christmas. She couldn't afford to buy new stuff to do that. She could barely afford to restock her inventory.

"We could award prizes," the chamber secretary offered.

They'd done that for their Christmas Shopper's Walk. Ginger had heard several complaints that the judging was biased. The same couple of businesses won every year regardless of the decorations used.

Ginger bounced the eraser top of her pencil against her notepad. "One prize, a really good one, and the judging should come from the community. Something they can be part of, like maybe anonymous online voting on the chamber website."

Brady narrowed his eyes. "We've already paid for our statewide advertising. That could be the grand prize. A year's worth of advertising across the state, as long as the Maple Springs Chamber of Commerce is somehow listed, too."

Ginger's mouth watered. She could barely afford to advertise, and then only with a few local print runs. Statewide exposure was definitely a grand prize. At least, it was for her. It might make a difference in her online sales, maybe even her summertime foot traffic.

"I like it!" Ginger finally said.

Brady clapped his hands together once. "Then let's get moving."

The sound startled the treasurer, who'd nodded off during the meeting.

"I'll let the bureau of tourism know our plans and invite them for the big reveal. Just maybe, with some hype, they'll send someone up here. If we can show Maple Springs as a place for lovers on Valentine's Day, we might have a shot at making the state campaign." Brady stood, looking thoughtful. "Yes, yes, that's our theme—Maple Springs Is for Lovers. Ginger, get the word out. Sandy, draft a newsletter today and email it. Let's get this done now!"

Ginger held up her hand. "Whoa, Brady. When will we announce the winner and how?"

He was pacing the floor of the small boardroom, clearly excited. "Maple Springs is *the* place for lovers. Let's prove that on Valentine's Day. We need something to draw couples downtown other than restaurant specials. But what?"

"Something romantic," Sandy said.

"I'm stumped." Ginger wasn't one for romantic daydreams. Men on white horses didn't exist in her world.

Brady laughed. "I rely on you ladies for that insight."

"My brother has one of those fancy horse-drawn carriages. Maybe we can hire him for the weekend." The treasurer yawned.

Brady grinned. "Perfect. Let's make it so."

Ginger shared a look with Sandy. This might actually work.

The area restaurants usually ran Valentine's Day specials, but they could ramp it up this year. And if the town's merchants cleared away their old Christmas greenery in exchange for hearts and cherubs, downtown would look fresh and pretty. With a town made over in time for Valentine's Day, they might even lure skiers away from the hills and into the shops. She'd have to find a Valentine's Day tea blend sure to spark romance.

Thoughts of Captain Zach and the way he'd held her tight this morning sent a shiver through her. Surely Zach's shop would open soon. Even so, Ginger needed to convince him along with the other merchants to decorate their storefronts in time for Valentine's Day with the theme that Maple Springs Is for Lovers.

She was used to cajoling store owners to buy into chamber-sponsored programs. But Zach Zelinsky was a much harder nut to crack. And grumpy, besides. If nothing else, her childhood had taught her to steer clear of men like him.

She'd have a greater chance of winning the grand prize if his window was decorated like hers. Both had to be good. And that meant they'd have to work together.

Her belly flipped. Anticipating *that* conversation wasn't pleasant. She might get a fight or all-out agreement, and she didn't know which one scared her more.

Chapter Two

Ginger entered her store through the back. Flicking on the lights, she heard muffled voices and froze, listening. The sound came from next door. She strode into her shop and peered through the sliding glass door that separated their respective spaces. Opened boxes were strewn everywhere and Bubble Wrap and packing peanuts puddled on the newly refinished wide-plank floor.

Curious for a peek at the kind of work an ex-army captain might make, Ginger couldn't stand it. Flicking the lock on her side, she tried the slider and it gave way to her touch. He hadn't locked his side. Her heels clicked on the wood floor as she entered, announcing her presence.

And Zach appeared from around a corner. "Oh, it's you."

Could he sound less enthused?

"It's me." She grinned at him. "The door was open and I, um, really wanted to see your work."

He cocked one eyebrow.

And Ginger felt her cheeks burn. Didn't he believe her? She wasn't being nosy without reason. She heard the sound of machine tinkering and looked beyond him. "Oh, but you have people. I'll just head back the way I came."

Zach waved them off. "Inspectors. I can show you around."

Ginger stepped forward and hit a piece of Bubble Wrap, causing a loud snap and pop.

Zach ducked. His gaze homed in sharp and deadly while his whole body tensed. He coiled like a spring ready for action. But this wasn't combat, nor was he under fire.

"Sorry." Ginger tried to shake off her unease, but his reaction proved his training must be hard to forget.

Maybe he carried things, dangerous things, deep inside still. She'd seen the documentaries on TV. Captain Zach was a civilian now, yet the sound of popping Bubble Wrap had gotten to him. Was that normal? Was he?

He called to the two inspectors who'd stepped out to see about the noise, as well. "Just Bubble

Wrap." Then Zach gave her his hand. "Come on, there are obstacles through here."

Okay, maybe she made too much of his reaction. She slipped her hand into his. His skin felt cold, clammy even, before heat radiated between them. It wasn't comforting. Not by a mile. It was all she could do to keep holding on. And holding on was a must because wide steps in the slim wool skirt she wore over black tights and heels was impossible.

He steered her around the cardboard land mines, but she still stumbled against the edge of a box. His grip tightened and he growled, "Careful."

Ginger's pulse sped and she pulled her hand away. Maybe if he hadn't dragged her like some caveman. She straightened and breathed deep. "I'll walk slower."

"Hmmph."

Seriously? She lifted her chin and glared right into his eyes. Big mistake. Captain Zach's eyes were blue. Really, really blue and mesmerizing. And he hadn't shaved, making him look even more rugged.

And powerful.

Ginger shivered. She needed to focus on the reasons why she didn't want to find him attractive. She forced a smile. But once she looked around, she forgot everything else. “Wow, you’ve really made a lot of changes.”

The corner of his mouth lifted, and then he was all business. “This is where it happens, or will once I’m given the A-OK.”

The changes to Sally’s shop had been huge. Walls had been taken out and the glassblowing studio part took up most of the space, leaving only a small area for retail displays. A wrought iron safety fence separated the two.

Her heart pinched. No more Sally, the elderly woman who’d taken Ginger under her wing. And no potter’s wheel in the corner by the back window. She was used to seeing Sally there, her hands covered with clay. In its place was a big steel table, a heavy workbench with rails and some freaky-looking tools and hot ovens. This place now looked like something out of an old horror movie.

“Scary.” She meant it.

Zach chuckled. “Hence the partition to keep my customers from wandering too close to the hot work.”

“Why more than one furnace?”

Zach pointed. “The large one is the tank furnace where the molten glass is kept. Next, the smaller round one is the glory hole. That’s used to reheat pieces I’m working on to keep the glass malleable. And then that over there is called an annealing oven. I'll use that once a piece is finished, to slowly cool it down to prevent shattering. That's the plan, anyway. And that's Sally's kiln. I'm not sure yet how I'll use it."

Apparently to get Captain Zach talking, all she needed to do was ask about his craft. "Have you unpacked any of your work?"

"Not yet."

Ginger glanced toward the men who must have interrupted him while he'd been opening boxes. "What about a name for your store?"

"ZZ Glassworks."

"Good ring to it." Ginger nodded. "Do you have a sign?"

He shrugged. "I might etch it on the window or door."

Ginger scanned the empty window that was exactly like hers and shook her head. "It'll get lost in your display."

"My display?"

"Your artwork. An outside sign would be better and easier to spot from the street. You'll want your window stocked with product to lure customers inside."

He narrowed his gaze. "Ah, yeah."

"I know a sign guy in town who'll give you a good deal."

He laughed then. A harsh bark of a sound. "Of course you do."

"What?" She settled her hands on her hips. Did he think she got a kickback or something for referring business? In a small town, shop owners looked out for each other. And recommended a deal if they could.

"Are you always this cheerfully helpful?"

"Pretty much. Are you always this grumpy?"

He chuckled. "Pretty much." Then he scanned her from head to toe. "You're taller today."

She lifted her foot. "It's the heels."

"I noticed." His voice lowered a smidgen, but disapproval shone from his eyes.

What? Didn't he like high heels? It wasn't as if he had to wear them. And then it dawned on her that just maybe he liked them a lot, especially on her.

Ginger checked her watch. Almost ten. She had to open. She had to get away from this new sense of awareness between them. "I better get back. Thanks for the tour."

Walking away, she swung back around. He'd made her forget all about the importance of the upcoming Valentine's Day contest. No time. "After you're settled in, we can chat more about your window display and the contest the chamber is sponsoring."

"Can't wait." His voice sounded flat.

Ginger felt her cheeks flare yet again, right along with her ire. The man might not talk much, but he sure got his message across.

Captain Zach did things *his* way.

She backed up and nearly tripped over another box.

Zach grabbed her arm to steady her.

She did a little growling of her own. Ginger needed to get back to her home base before she made a bigger fool of herself. "Thanks."

"It's the heels." He gave her platforms of black suede a pointed look.

"I found them at a thrift store," she blurted.

Not that it was any of his business how she spent her money, but she didn't want her landlord to think she spent frivolously. Maybe because when she was a kid coming home with an expensive treasure she'd found for a song, she'd had to explain her actions. How many times had she played defense to her father's offense? Her mother had finally warned her not to let Dad see them for fear of an argument.

Ginger escaped through the glass slider, closed it behind her with a soft click and blew out her breath.

What was the deal with Zach Zelinsky?

He sure wasn't a chatty guy, and that made her wonder why he'd gone into retail. And why'd he make her so nervous with his gruff ways? She wasn't a clumsy person, but around him she couldn't keep solid footing. The man was definitely intimidating. And Ginger did not like to be intimated.

That evening, Zach knocked on the sliding glass door. Ginger had kept it locked throughout the day, and he was glad since he'd been in and out all afternoon. That locked door had kept her few customers from spilling into his space. Several had peered in at him while he'd unloaded boxes, though. Passing his furnace inspections had been the last of the paperwork required before he could finally open his doors. All he needed to do was finish stocking the shelves and then start making new glass.

She walked to the slider and unlocked her side. Opening the door, she peered up at him with those big brown eyes of hers. "Hey."

"Are you closed?"

She nodded. "Yup. This time of year I'm open Tuesday through Saturday, ten to six."

"Good hours." He liked having two days off in row and might as well be open the same times as her.

"I open Mondays, too, starting in May for summer hours. But I'm always closed Sunday."

"Day of rest?"

"That and church." She smiled.

He needed to find the right church, but he had time to figure it out. "I've unpacked, if you're still interested."

He wasn't being nice. He wanted to see her reaction to his glasswork. Was it good enough? She seemed to know a lot about running a gift shop and the expectations of local customers.

"Absolutely." Her pretty eyes gleamed. "Do you know how hard it was not to press my nose against this glass door like my customers?"

He chuckled and stepped aside. She'd had two elderly women in her store, and they had indeed pressed their noses on the glass and watched him unpack.

He'd utilized most of the clear shelving that came with the shop but had arranged it differently—out in the open instead of up against the walls, giving the small retail space an artsy feel like the studio where he'd apprenticed and learned the trade.

He watched her closely as she walked around his displays, her slender fingertips gently touching glass ornaments and bowls. She was careful, but thorough. Was she putting him on, looking *that* interested?

"Wow." Ginger stopped and stared at one of his few glass sculptures. It was a twisted mass of smoky glass with a dash of red at its center that glowed from the light he'd installed underneath it. "How'd you come up with this?"

He shrugged.

Emotions had a way of working their way in while he shaped glass. He'd been running on empty when he'd made that particular sculpture. Frustrated and angry after a long deployment, he'd clung to a sliver of hope from a Bible scripture he'd read from the book of Jeremiah. He'd memorized verse eleven of chapter twenty-nine and had held on to its promise. He'd even chanted it when things got rough in the field.

For I know the thoughts that I think toward you, says the LORD, thoughts of peace and not of evil, to give you a future and a hope.

"This is so beautiful." She looked at him in awe. As if she couldn't believe he'd made it.

"Thanks." Sometimes, he couldn't believe it either.

Ginger's hair was a riot of red curls that caressed her shoulders. A live flame she was, radiating warmth. It seared like a pipe burn, this pull she had on him. Or maybe more like a backyard campfire luring him near, daring him to pull up a log and relax. But even campfires burned if a person got too close.

She nodded toward the workshop. "When will you make new stuff?"

"Soon."

"Well, that's real specific." Even her sarcasm came across sweet.

"How 'bout I let you know."

Her eyes widened with surprise at the sharpness of his retort. He hadn't meant to sound so surly.

She didn't miss a beat, though, and didn't back down. "Yeah, you do that because I'd love to see how it's done."

Great.

But then, what did he expect? Blowing glass was a cool process. So why did the idea of Ginger watching him work make his skin itch?

She looked at him, curious. "How long have you been doing this?"

Zach scratched his temple. "Maybe ten years?"

"All while in the army?"

"Yeah."

What started as an art class became a hobby, a creative release and then a place to forget. He'd had his studio plans drawn up well before he'd moved back home. Before he'd even found a building. Before he'd been RIFed. He'd always known how he wanted his shop laid out with an open space so his workshop was in full view of the buying public. He wanted to keep an eye on his store while working. Still, he hadn't expected to become a shop owner this soon in life.

"But how? I mean when did you find the time?"

"I learned during downtime, when I was off duty."

"Oh." She didn't look satisfied. She looked ready to ask more questions.

Zach didn't want to answer questions. "I've got to cut this short."

He'd promised his mom he'd make it for dinner. And he needed to move the last of his things into the apartment above.

"Oh. Sorry. Thanks for showing me around." She smiled, hesitated to leave. "I still have to fill you in on the window display contest."

"Sure. No problem. Another time?"

She nodded. "I'll hold you to that."

"Okay. See ya later." He was halfway tempted to invite her along so she could tell him on the way, but that might send the wrong message. He watched her click her way across the wood floor and slip back through the slider into her tea shop. Ginger Carleton was pretty. A pretty, church-going woman.

But too young. Too young for him.

A few days later, Ginger peered into Zach's studio. He'd been open less than a week, but shoppers swarmed. Curiosity drove a lot of traffic, but folks purchased product, too, and Zach had made sales. A lot of sales.

She spotted him surrounded by three women, and Captain Zach looked like a trapped wolf ready to snap or chew off his own paw any second now to escape.

He glanced her way and waved her in. Not a welcoming I've-got-something-to-show-you wave, more like a get-over-here-now-I-need-you sort of wave.

Ginger clenched her jaw. She shouldn't covet his customers, but she did. Some had wandered into her shop, but most didn't. No matter how frustrating it was watching shoppers snub their noses at her tea, it wasn't Zach's fault. And ignoring his plea for help might not bode well for renewing her lease come the end of the year.

At this point in her shop-owning career, she shouldn't need an indefinite rental agreement, but that's what she'd had with Sally. Ginger felt sold out right along with the building.

But it was Sally's building to sell, and the woman was well past retirement age. Ginger should be standing on her own two feet by now, not relying on her mentor's charity. Not filled with envy because Zach's studio had been hopping while hers barely took a few steps. And even fewer sales.

Reality had a way of taking a sharp bite out of her plans when she least expected it. Taking a deep breath, she rallied her sweetest smile and headed his way. “Can I help?”

A look of genuine relief washed over his face. “Gift wrap?”

“I’ve got some.” She ducked back into her shop and returned with a pile of floral tissue paper and ribbon. More shoppers accosted Zach, so she went a step further. “I can help you at the counter, ladies.”

Zach gave her a grateful half smile.

And Ginger’s heart did a little flip right along with her belly.

Uh-oh.

She swallowed the bitter pill of unwanted attraction and scolded herself besides. Really? Ginger herded the heavily perfumed women with glass ornaments in hand to Zach’s small counter. Underneath were boxes and rolls of Bubble Wrap. She worked quickly, boxing up the glass treasures. It was easy to swirl tissue paper around the box and secure it with ribbon and a pouf of tissue on top. Nice.

Hunting under the counter once more, Ginger found plain paper bags and Zach’s cash box. Inside the locked box with the key still hanging in the lock, she found a phone with an adapter to slide credit cards for payment.

While she checked out the women's purchases, Zach discussed a custom order with two other women. She overheard parts of the conversation and surmised that they wanted a larger version of his lit smoky glass sculpture. They wanted a unique chandelier in their waiting room.

From the chamber office, Ginger knew all about the medical office geared specifically for women that would open sometime in the summer. Obviously, the doctors wanted softer lighting than fluorescent overheads for their clients.

Ginger peeked at Zach. He stood tall and handsome in jeans and a loose cotton sweater. Even in plain clothes, he had that stiff military bearing. A figure of austere authority.

The women offered Zach a business card and a check as down payment on a piece they didn't care how long it took to finish. After they'd left he turned toward her. "Thank you."

Ginger waved off his gratitude. "Custom order?"

"A big one." He looked grim.

"That's good news, right?"

"Not if I don't have time or the help to make it. I've never made anything that big."

Was she supposed to feel sorry for him? So far, his opening week was proving to be a success. "You're going to have to get some gift wrap. Especially with Valentine's Day coming up."

"Why's that?"

Ginger rolled her eyes. Did she have to spell it out? "Haven't you ever bought a girl flowers or chocolates for Valentine's Day?"

He shrugged. "No. Not much of a Valentine's Day guy."

No surprise there. "Well, other people do, right along with specialty gifts like yours and mine. You'll need to be ready because we've got a lot planned."

"We?"

She took a deep breath. Finally, she'd roll out the details of the window display contest. She'd helped him out so he sort of owed her. "The chamber of commerce. I'm their liaison with the merchants." Ginger stood a little straighter. "Since Valentine's Day falls on a Saturday this year, we're hyping it up big-time. We want to catch the bureau of tourism's attention. Maple Springs might even be highlighted in the state of Michigan ad campaign if we can get everyone on board. Part of that is running a window display contest among the downtown merchants and businesses. The winner will be announced on Valentine's Day."

One eyebrow rose. "Right, the contest. What's the prize?"

Ginger narrowed her gaze. She'd been trying to catch him for days to spell it all out. But he'd been busy. Maybe that lag time had finally sparked his interest. "A year's worth of statewide advertising already paid for by the chamber, as long as the chamber is listed, too."

He harrumphed. "Not interested."

And maybe not. Clearly, he didn't get it. "Well, I want to win. And to do that, I'm going to need your help."

His expression looked sharp enough to slice her in two. "How?"

She pointed toward their storefront. "We have identical windows. I think one of us would have a better chance of winning if they're tied together somehow. But it has to support the contest theme."

"Theme?" He looked amused now.

Ginger felt her face heat. "Maple Springs Is for Lovers."

Zach laughed.

And Ginger experienced a strong urge to belt him. "Why's that so funny?"

"That's hokey."

"It is not!" Ginger placed her hands on her hips. "The downtown restaurants will offer romantic dinner specials and the chamber is sponsoring horse-drawn carriage rides. All the merchants, if they're smart, will take advantage of the holiday, as well."

He snorted. "Valentine's Day was made up by the greeting card companies. It's no holiday."

"It's good business." She wasn't particularly fond of the day either, having been stuck at home more times than not, but it made for sales opportunities. "I make up gift baskets with romantic teas and aromatic spices."

Zach looked as if it was all a game.

Maybe it seemed silly to him. He'd seen combat, probably had made life-and-death decisions, but this contest—and the advertising campaign win—might mean the life or death of her shop!

She crooked her finger at him. "Come with me."

He gave her a curious look but did as she asked. He followed her through the slider into her store. She slipped behind her counter, where her laptop lay opened, and refreshed her page. He leaned over the counter to see her screen as she clicked around. That wasn't going to work.

"Come around so I can show you what I'm talking about." Ginger quickly went through the state of Michigan's seasonal tourism ads. "See all these little towns? They're real and I want Maple Springs to be one of them. This year, we have a chance, if I can get everyone on board with the contest."

He peered over her shoulder as she played several commercials. She felt the warmth of him standing behind her, and every cell in her body seemed to stand at attention and take notice. She'd been on her own for so long, struggling to make something of herself with only Sally's support. But Sally had not only retired, she moved away to be near her son and grandkids.

What would it feel like to have someone else looking out for her? Helping her succeed instead of laughing at her efforts.

"So, that's the real prize—statewide recognition?"

"Yeah." She turned and bumped into his arm.

He quickly stepped back, out of her way.

She looked up at him. "Are you in?"

"In?"

Ginger let out a huff of frustration. "The window contest."

He sighed. "I don't know. When does it have to be up?"

"The week before Valentine's Day."

He looked really grim then. "That's right around the corner."

She clenched her fists. "We've got a little over three weeks. Plenty of time."

He rubbed his chin. "We'll see."

Before Ginger could press harder, the door to his shop opened with the ring of the bells he'd installed. From her counter, she had an open view of his retail space, but most of his workshop area was out of sight. Two customers made their way into his studio and looked around.

"Gotta go." Zach headed for his side and slipped through the slider.

Ginger easily overheard their *oohs* and *ahhs*, but once the two young women saw the man responsible for making the glass items, their eyes grew round with interest. Feminine giggles and titters grew louder as they grilled Zach with questions and pretty much fawned all over him.

Ginger shook her head at his one-word answers. The man practically spoke in grunts and growls.

Really, he needed to improve his store-side demeanor lest he get an unwelcoming reputation. Not a good thing for a shop owner dependent on the public's buying habits. People in Maple Springs talked, and talk spread fast. She should warn Zach about that. But then, he'd grown up here. He should know.

Watching him back away from the two women, she got the impression that Captain Zach wasn't real comfortable with feminine attention. He'd never be taken for a flirt, that was for sure.

And that made Ginger smile.

Chapter Three

Saturday morning, Zach looked over his receipts. His first full week after opening his doors and he'd done pretty well. Even had a couple of custom orders to work on. He spotted his sister Monica taking pictures outside and gritted his teeth. She'd been after him to set up a website.

She popped her head in the door. "Hi."

He waved her in.

"Wow, nice." She took a couple more pictures and snapped one of him.

"Must you?"

"Yes. Now show me around."

Zach glanced at Ginger waiting on an elderly customer in her own shop. He could hear her chipper voice chatting about the weather and so-and-so's son in college while scooping funny-looking tea leaves into plastic baggies.

She hadn't a care in the world. Ginger was that way. She put her customers at ease and made retail look effortless.

She put him at ease and got under his skin at the same time.

"You two getting along okay?" his sister asked.

"Yeah, why?" Zach opened the wrought iron gate that separated his workspace from the retail portion of his studio.

Monica followed him. "You were scowling at her."

"That's just how I look." Like it or not, Ginger was a fireball of sunny energy who'd pushed her way into his thoughts more often than not. He found her too attractive for his own good but couldn't quite figure her out. "So, what's her story?"

"Story?" His sister didn't understand.

"You know her. And her shop. I haven't seen many customers in there this week. Does she have a good product?"

Monica shrugged. "Yeah. Good enough, I suppose, but the new coffee shop in town started selling loose tea as well as coffee beans. I think she's taken a hit from the competition."

"Huh." Zach thought about how Ginger never left her store. Even at lunchtime, she'd heat up something in the microwave instead of go out.

They kept the glass slider between their shops open during store hours. And Ginger graciously watched over his place whenever he stepped out, but he'd never had the opportunity to return the favor. Maybe she didn't trust him to take care of her customers. He couldn't say he blamed her. He'd never been good at all that inane chatter.

"You've done a nice job here, Zach. I'll do a mock-up for you to review and then we can talk about content." Monica placed her camera in her purse.

"Thanks." He meant it, too. He appreciated her doing all this for free.

She looked thoughtful. "You're my big brother, and I'm glad you came home in one piece. I owe you."

Zach shifted. He didn't deserve to be home in one piece. If that RPG had hit only a few inches to the right, he'd have been in a body bag. "You don't."

His sister grabbed his arm and squeezed. "We all do."

He looked up as Ginger entered through the open slider. Her burnished hair had been swooped up into a bouncy tail that swayed when she walked.

"Hi, Monica." Ginger's makeup was always

applied with a light hand, but this morning her lips were the color of ripe berries.

"Morning." His sister checked her watch. "Sorry, no time to chat. I have to meet Brady and set up the online voting for the window display contest. You two have fun."

After his sister left, Zach turned his attention to Ginger. Not hard to do. She caught his eye often enough. "Hey."

She leaned against his checkout counter. "So, have you thought about the window display?"

He raised the now half-empty mug of coffee that she'd made him before they'd opened. "Is that why you brought me this?"

She grinned, clearly guilty as charged and not a bit sorry. "You don't like tea, so coffee works better than vinegar."

"What?"

"You know the old saying about catching more bees with honey than vinegar? That coffee is my honey."

"I see." He ran a hand through his hair in an attempt to stop dwelling on those plump berry-tinted lips of hers. Honey might pale in sweetness. He'd know with one taste.

And that'd cause all kinds of trouble.

He scanned his front window. Following her example, he'd hung up a few glass ornaments and even placed a bowl of multicolored globes on a stand so people could get a quick look through the window, but that was pretty much it.

Ginger's window was a riot of hanging teapots over a small café table set with another teapot and cups and even a couple of stuffed teddy bears. He didn't know what bears had to do with anything, but whatever. She'd also made a small shelving unit out of wooden milk crates that was littered with spice bottles and decorative tins. There was more going on in her window than her shop.

"That sign isn't going to cut it." She pointed to the lower corner.

"It's fine for now," he growled. Give the woman an inch and she'd take a mile.

He'd made his own sign on the computer and then slipped it into a clear plastic sign holder that he'd picked up at an office supply store. He needed to focus on making new items and custom work, not mess with a window display. Juggling customer interruptions with glassblowing wasn't easy. Most days, he waited until after hours to make anything new.

At this rate, he'd never accommodate the big orders, or remake his own overhead lighting with blown glass globes as he wanted. But he wasn't prepared to hire help just yet and he didn't have time to bring on an apprentice. A real catch-22.

"What about glass hearts?" Ginger said. "I've ordered a few heart-shaped teapots that I may hang in my window."

Did it really matter? Either people would check out his store or not. "Actually, I've made a few."

Her eyes gleamed as if she were a kid in a candy store. "Can I see?"

He chuckled. "Most are still in the annealer, but I have some ready—"

The door jingled and his brother, followed by the woman who he assumed was his fiancée, stepped inside with a swirl of cold air and snowflakes.

"Nice digs." Matthew glanced around the space with admiration. "Zach, this is Annie. We thought we'd stop in and see the place."

He extended his hand. "Good to meet you. And this is—"

"Oh, we know each other." Ginger waved him off. "Where's the baby?"

"With Marie," Annie said.

"That's Grandma," Ginger clarified. "Your brother used to work with Annie's late husband."

Zach nodded. He'd heard as much from his mom after he'd come home. Annie was two years older than Zach, but didn't look it. Not at all.

"You have a beautiful shop, Zach. Are you glad to be home?" Annie asked.

His gaze strayed to Ginger while he thought about the question. "Yeah, sure."

"Well, thank you for your service. You do Maple Springs proud." Annie meant it, too. No lip service there.

"Honored." He gave her a nod because it's what he did. Accept thanks and move on.

Many had thanked him at the parade and a few customers had stopped in to do the same. He gave them the standard awkward response he'd given his future sister-in-law. He didn't feel so honored anymore. More like discarded. Chewed up and spit out because his usefulness was over.

Logically, he knew it couldn't be because he'd lost good men in that ambush. That happened three years ago, but had it played a role? Or maybe because he'd come up from the enlisted ranks. Did it really matter why the army chose to cut him loose?

It would to his father. Zach had been part of the latest round of defense budget cuts, and regardless of the reason, bottom line, he hadn't been worth keeping.

Annie nodded toward the opened slider. "Ginger, can I get some tea?"

"Sure thing." Ginger followed without a backward glance.

Zach watched the women make their exit, momentarily mesmerized by one red ponytail.

"She's coming to Mom and Dad's."

"What's that?"

Matthew studied the glass sculptures. "Tonight. Ginger is Annie's best friend, so I invited her."

"How old is she?" Zach regretted blurting that out when he saw the stormy look on his brother's face. "I meant Ginger."

"Thirty-two, I think. My age."

Zach was floored. "You sure about that?"

His brother laughed. "Don't worry, she's old enough."

"Yeah?" Zach shook his head to clear it. "Not that it matters."

"Uh-huh." Matthew clearly wasn't convinced.

Zach peered through the glass slider at Ginger, and then quickly looked away. He slapped his younger brother on the back. "Come on, I'll show you the rest of the shop."

During the quick tour, Zach's mind kept wandering back to Ginger. She was young, but not *that* young. Not off-limits young as he'd first thought. And that made her even more alluring. But romance with Ginger would be navigating an entirely different kind of minefield. He might not lose a limb, but losing one's heart could be equally painful.

He wasn't in the mood to become that kind of casualty. Right now, he had enough to deal with.

"So, what do you think?" Annie asked.

Ginger inhaled the earthy scents of citrus and cinnamon while shoveling loose tea leaves into a plastic bag. "About what?"

Annie wiggled her eyebrows. "Your new *landlord*."

Ginger concentrated on closing up the bag. She knew exactly what Annie wanted but tried playing dumb. "Ugh, that's right. February's rent is due soon."

"Nice dodge."

Ginger secured the metallic twisty-tie with fascinated interest.

"You like him, don't you?" Annie zeroed in better than a hawk circling a squirrel.

Ginger sighed. "No, I do not. He's touchy, downright grumpy and cantankerous besides. But look at him."

Annie did just that. Maybe a little longer than Ginger thought necessary. "The Zelinsky men are handsome, I'll give you that." Running her finger along the counter, Annie stalled. "Matthew says Zach can be pretty intense. Sooooo..."

"So what?" Ginger hissed.

Annie's pretty blue eyes widened with amusement. "Maybe he needs someone positive. Someone like you."

Ginger shrugged. She'd caught a look or two from Zach that was intriguing. And that morning he'd kept her from falling flat on her backside had been interesting, too. And nerve rattling.

He was not only her landlord, but a neighboring store owner. Acting on her attraction would be tricky at best and not very smart. If they got involved and the relationship went south, Ginger wouldn't stick around. She'd bolt. Even with Zach's increased rent, this was the cheapest place in town. She didn't want to lose her business because of a bad romantic entanglement.

And something about the surly Captain Zach screamed *bad romantic entanglement.*

Annie dug for a twenty from her purse to pay for the tea. "Are you still going tonight?"

Ginger counted back the change. "Tonight?"

"Dinner party at the Zelinskys', remember? Matthew said you'd agreed to go."

"Oh, yeah. I forgot for a minute, but I'll be there."

If Annie needed her, Ginger wasn't about to let her down, even though she'd promised before she'd thought it through. Before she'd felt this twitchiness toward Zach.

At home would he smile more? Laugh, even? She didn't want to miss that. But then again, maybe she should.

"Maybe you and Zach can ride together."

"Right." But Ginger's stomach flipped. That'd be awkward.

Matthew joined them, looking antsy to leave. "Ready?"

"We're going to lunch where we're having the wedding. Final details and all that," Annie explained.

"Have fun." Ginger glanced at Matthew and laughed. He didn't look as if he cared about details. He looked like a man who wanted to get married. She walked them to the door and waved as they left.

A throng of customers had come in while Annie and Matthew were in her store. Not locals, but tourists—skiers maybe, obviously up for the weekend. They looked over Zach's work. Some picked up an ornament or two and were ready to buy them. Where was he?

Ginger made a move toward the shoppers

when Zach appeared with a basket of small multicolored glass hearts. He gave her a nod and placed the basket on his checkout counter.

The three women in the store hurried over.

"These are so cute," one said.

"Adorable."

"How much?"

Zach hesitated. "Uh, ten."

"I'll take four."

Ginger hoped they wouldn't clean him out before she got a look at them. But then more customers came in and some wanted tea. Then Brady from the chamber stopped by to check on her progress with the local merchants, and by the time Ginger had a chance to scoot back over to Zach's shop, it was closing time. Her favorite time of the day.

She locked her front door, watched the snow fall beneath the illumination of the streetlamps outside and sighed. Today had been a pretty good day for sales. And pathetic when she considered four measly purchases a good day.

"Tired?" Zach leaned against the slider, basket in hand. His eyes looked red, as if maybe he'd missed a night's sleep. He looked tired, yet asked about her.

"Not too bad. What about you?"

"I'm tired of waiting on customers."

Ginger laughed. "Better get used to it."

"Yeah." He held out the basket. "Here."

She inched closer and peeked inside. Only four glass hearts remained. "For me?"

"You've really helped me out." His deep voice caressed her ears. "Thanks."

Ginger pulled out one small red heart with a clear loop at the top. "Well, thank you. You're not charging enough for these, by the way."

Zach shrugged. "Take them all. I'll make more. They're not hard to do."

"This one is fine. I haven't seen you blow glass. When are you making things?"

"Evenings and sometimes late at night."

"No wonder you're tired," Ginger teased.

A shadow crossed over his features but was gone as quickly as it had appeared. "I'll figure it out."

Did she imagine that haunted look?

Ginger clutched the pretty glass heart in her hand. "Thanks for this. I think you should use these in your window."

"Again with the window. You're like a dog on a bone."

She made a face. Maybe Zach was all bark. He'd given her a heart and that felt pretty good.

He shifted his stance and then cleared his throat. "I understand you've been invited to my folks' party."

Ginger's heart raced. "Yes."

"Are you going?" His blue eyes pierced hers.

Didn't he want her to? Surely, Annie would understand if she bailed at the last minute. "Uh…"

"If you are, ride with me." That sounded more like an order than a request.

"I can drive." Did Captain Zach think she couldn't manage on her own? It was only ten miles away.

Ginger glanced at the snow piling up on the sidewalks out front. The forecast called for heavy bands of lake effect through the night. "I mean, I don't want to put you out. I have to be up early in the morning, so I can only stay for a bit."

"I won't be long." His voice sounded so stern and irritated. "No sense both of us driving in this weather."

She looked into his tired blue eyes and found herself nodding. "Okay, but I have to change. What time do you want to leave?"

"An hour."

"Deal." Ginger reached out to pull the slider closed.

Zach stopped her. "This isn't a date or anything."

She tipped her head. Good grief, did he want her to go or not? "I don't have to go?"

"That's not what I meant."

Ginger placed her hands on her hips. "Then what did you mean?"

His eyes narrowed, but he raised his hands in surrender. "Nothing. Forget it."

Yeah, right. "Fine."

"Good. I'll see you in an hour."

Ginger closed the slider with a hard snap.

What a jerk! Not a date. Seriously? He's the one who had asked her; she hadn't asked to ride along.

She closed up her shop and stomped upstairs to change. Well, at least it wouldn't be a long night ahead, but the drive there and back promised to be a real treat.

An hour later, Zach knocked on the door to Ginger's apartment above her shop. This felt an awful lot like a date. And he'd made it worse by trying to point out the obvious. He didn't want to date his tenant. Didn't want to send the wrong message, either.

Ginger opened the door wide. Her hair looked the same, but she'd changed into jeans and a bulky knit sweater. It didn't matter what she wore, or how she fixed her hair. What made her most attractive was the light that shone from within her. That fire. Ginger had a glow all her own.

"Hey." Even her cheerful voice warmed him.

"Can I come in?"

"Sure." Wariness crept into her eyes, but she backed up and let him enter.

"I didn't get a good look at your place before I bought the building." He looked around. "Your apartment is nicer than mine."

Her gaze narrowed as if trying to read between the lines of what he said.

Great. "Don't worry, I'm not going to kick you out. Just saying you made it nice."

"I'm the queen of thrift stores and yard sales."

She wasn't afraid to use color. The walls were painted a sunny yellow and the tall windows had vibrant floral-patterned curtains instead of the plain wood blinds he used. Even the cupboards in her galley kitchen had been painted brick red.

He spotted the glass heart he'd given her hanging in the window by yellow ribbon to secure it. "You hung it up."

She cocked her head to one side. "Did you think I'd smash it or something?"

"I apologize for earlier. I just wanted to be clear." He smiled then, hoping she understood.

She shook her head without any sign of a

grudge. "I see why you're not a Valentine's kind of guy."

He laughed at her comeback. "You have no idea."

It hit him then that he didn't want to go to his parents' party. He'd rather stay right here and curl up with Ginger on that plush couch against the far wall to watch a movie. His comment about tonight not being a date wasn't really for her benefit but his own.

A reminder that Ginger Carleton was off-limits. Or should be.

"Ready?"

"Almost." She sat down and pulled on knee-high leather boots over a pair of fuzzy striped socks. Then she slipped into a down jacket, more fuzzy mittens and a scarf. Grabbing her purse, she looked up. "I'm ready."

He held the door open and followed down the stairs and outside. The snow fell harder now and the wind had kicked up, biting his nose with bitter cold.

"Is your car good in the snow?" She eyed his Jeep Wrangler with doubt.

"I have four-wheel drive, so yes. And the clearance is higher than your Beetle."

She nodded and climbed in, kicking snow from her feet before swinging them inside.

He started the engine and brushed off the

windows before slipping behind the wheel. Glancing at Ginger huddled in the seat next to him, looking cold, her couch beckoned even louder. "So, what's going on in the morning? Church?"

"What?" She had the look of sweet confusion, as if he'd interrupted a pleasant daydream. "Oh. I volunteer on the worship team at church, and tomorrow is my Sunday to sing. I have to get there early to practice."

He wasn't the least bit surprised that Ginger was truly a woman of faith. Maybe having faith in common was what drew him. "Do you sing solo?"

"No way!" Ginger chuckled. "I'm not that good, but I can carry a tune well enough I suppose, or they would have tossed me by now. There are a few of us who sing with a small band. Do you go to church?"

"Yes." He pulled out onto the road. "But I haven't found what I'm looking for."

"Would you like to go with me? I mean, you know, check it out." She looked surprised for inviting him.

All things considered, he was, too. He couldn't resist teasing her. "Are you asking me out?"

She's old enough.

Her cheeks flushed. "Uh, no. You made that pretty clear."

Had he really hurt her feelings? If so, it was a small price to pay for keeping things safe between them. "I'm your landlord."

She gave him a cool stare. "Yeah, I know. Wait, don't you go where your parents attend?"

"I'm looking for something less traditional." He'd gone only once since he came home, and the church he'd grown up attending didn't fit anymore.

She fumbled in her purse for a second or two. Then she whipped out a business card and placed it in his drink holder. "I go to Maple Springs Community Church and the service starts at nine. That's the address and phone number. You can meet me there, since I'm going in early. It's just a couple miles heading south, out of town."

He nodded. "You're quite the promoter, aren't you?"

She shrugged but looked as if she braced for a slam.

He hadn't meant to sound so critical and was sorry for it. "I have a proposition for you."

She let loose a nervous-sounding giggle. "What's that?"

It might serve both their needs, for now. "You want to win that window contest, right?"

She gave him a pointed look.

He chuckled. "I don't have time to do it, but I'll give you free rein on both windows and pay for the materials if you'll do one thing."

Now she looked nervous. "What's that?"

"Wait on my customers so I can blow glass."

Her eyes narrowed.

"You get the prize no matter which window wins." He had to concentrate on the road ahead of him, but he could *feel* her weighing the pros and cons as she considered his request. He clenched his jaw to keep from coaxing her to accept. If what Monica had said was true, she could probably use the money.

"Okay, it's a deal." Ginger slipped off her mitten and held out her hand. "But we have to shake on it."

"What?"

"Make it a true agreement between shop owners. Unless you'd rather put it in writing?"

"We don't need to go that far." He grabbed her hand for a quick pump but didn't let go right away. Her skin felt soft. And something about the way her slender hand fit within his own made him feel protective of her. "We good?"

She pulled her hand away but wouldn't look at him. "We're good."

Hopefully, he'd get more work done. And with Miss Sunny-Smiles working his customers, hopefully he'd make more sales, too. Which meant hired help or an apprentice might not be far off. Down the road, he'd like to take over the whole building so he could accommodate bigger orders. That would mean even more help.

He glanced at Ginger looking out her window. Snow fell fast, keeping his speed low. He'd give her plenty of notice to move her shop when the time came. Unless—would she consider working for him? She was great with his customers, but then she'd be even more off-limits.

There might come a day when he wouldn't renew her business part of the lease. But if he hired Ginger Carleton, he'd have to give up any notions of cuddling on her couch.

Chapter Four

"Ginger, what a nice surprise." Helen Zelinsky's smile grew wider. "And you came with Zach."

"His Jeep has better clearance than my car, and the snow's really coming down out there." Ginger handed over her snow-dampened coat as if proving her appearance with Zach was about the weather and convenience. Nothing more.

She'd brushed off the snow as best she could on the front porch before coming inside. She'd helped Zach do the same and it had taken effort to keep her mitten-encased hands from lingering on his broad shoulders.

What would Zach have done had she hugged him for his offer to pay for her window display? After their mutual and rather awkward agreement about not dating, it would have been a stitch to see the look on his face. Still, she had the better deal, as waiting on his customers in addition to hers would be a snap this time of year.

"You know each other?" Zach gave his mom a kiss on the forehead. A soft show of respect.

And Ginger's heart twisted. In her family there was so little of that. They'd grown up learning to avoid conflict at all cost. As a result, respect and honesty were lost in an attempt to keep the peace. But there'd never been real peace at the Carletons'.

"Ginger helps with the church blood drives every quarter. She makes sure the volunteers get fed lunch."

"You make them food?" He cocked one eyebrow.

Ginger shook her head. "No, no. I pick up and deliver is all."

"Don't let her fool you. Each year, she organizes the downtown restaurants that donate, then picks up and delivers."

Ginger shrugged. "It's good business recognition for the local eateries and keeps the volunteers happy to come back. Everyone wins."

"Uh-huh." Zach had that scowl on his face again.

Now what?

"With this weather, I don't expect a big turnout tonight." Helen patted her son's chest, but she spoke to Ginger. "And that'll make Zach happy. You two go warm up by the fire. Dinner will be ready shortly."

Zach nodded but his face still looked grim.

She leaned toward him. "Why so glum? Don't you like parties?"

"Not really." He placed his hand against the middle of her back and steered her forward as more people came inside. His eyes softened into a look of tender concern. "You're involved in everything, aren't you?"

That look floored her. Was he was worried about her? It felt nice. The warm pressure of his touch did, too. Maybe too nice. She turned, forcing his hand to drop away. "Not everything, but enough. So, a grand opening event is probably not on your to-do list."

"Uh, no."

She laughed. "I could organize it for you."

He gave her a mock look of horror. "I'm sure you could. You seem to have the whole town organized."

She laughed again. "Not quite, but I'm working on it."

The corner of his mouth lifted in that semismile of his. "Want something to drink?"

"Sure."

"Hey, Ginger." Zach's sister Monica stood

in front of them. "I didn't get a chance to talk much this morning. So how's business?"

"Slow this time of year, you know, the usual." Ginger noticed that Zach had paid particular attention to how she answered. She didn't want her landlord worried about whether or not he'd get paid.

"I'm setting up Zach's website. Maybe we can chat about redoing your site, too, if you're interested."

"Thanks, but I'll stick with what I have for now." Ginger knew the quality of Monica's work. She maintained the chamber website. But Ginger couldn't afford a new site.

Not too many customers ordered from her online, besides. Those who did had first been in her store and signed up for her online newsletter. Tea and spices were sensory purchases. People liked to smell and taste before they bought. But with the contest win, with statewide exposure, all that could change.

Monica gestured toward Zach. "I finally talked him into one."

"Keep it simple," Zach grumbled.

Monica rolled her eyes. "Welcome home, grumpy-bear." Then she wiggled her eyebrows and whispered to Ginger, "Maybe you can soften him up."

Ginger felt her cheeks heat and glanced quickly at Zach.

He had to have heard his sister's comment and certainly looked like a bear roused from hibernation too soon. Needless to say, he wasn't amused by his sister's teasing. Or maybe the idea of her "softening him up." "Come on, the kitchen is this way."

Monica gave them a wide grin and a finger-fluttering wave. "Toodles."

Maybe coming tonight wasn't such a good idea. Both Monica and Helen believed she was Zach's date; probably the rest of his family did, too. And she hadn't even seen Annie yet. What if the person she came for stayed away because of the weather?

It wasn't far to the kitchen, but they ran into more family on the way, which meant more introductions.

"This is Ginger Carleton. She runs the tea shop next to mine." Zach nodded toward a blonder version of himself. "My brother Cam, and that's Darren over there."

Ginger smiled. She'd met Darren before. "Hello."

"And my father, Andy Zelinsky."

"How are you, sir?" Ginger shook his father's hand.

"Good to see you again, Ginger. Glad you

could make it." He slapped Zach on the back and wandered away.

After more meet and greets with cousins, aunts, uncles and family friends, they finally made it to the fridge. Zach filled her glass with iced tea and handed it over. "You know my parents pretty well."

Ginger shrugged. "Everyone knows your parents. They volunteer in town and then there's the syrup."

"Ah, yes, the Zelinsky syrup."

"Don't tell me you don't like maple syrup." He'd be worse than a bear if he didn't.

"I love it."

"But?" She sipped her iced tea and waited.

"But nothing. Real maple syrup reminds me of home."

"And that's a bad thing?" she asked.

He shrugged, but his eyes looked haunted.

Ginger stared at the ice in her glass. Not a whole lot she could say to that quick kill of the conversation.

More friends and relatives came into the kitchen, and they mauled Zach with praise and questions about his tours of duty. He answered with clipped sentences and brief descriptions. With a tight smile, Zach gripped a sturdy mug of coffee so hard, his knuckles had turned white.

Puzzling. These people were his relatives, his friends, and yet Zach seemed uncomfortable around them. She knew bad things happened in war, but had something horrific happened to Zach? Was it something he could handle?

Ginger's gut tightened. Was it something she could handle? She already cared. Maybe too much. And that scared her, too.

"We won't make it home tonight." Zach peered out the dining room window at the blowing snow. The wind howled and whipped more snow from the rooftop in long whirling tails of white. He glanced at Ginger standing beside him, cradling a cup of hot tea. "You okay with that?"

She looked outside and scrunched her nose. "Not much of a choice."

Being snowed in with Ginger had its advantages. Snuggling by the fire and maybe even roasting a few marshmallows came to mind, but not when most of his immediate family and a few cousins were stuck here, too. Didn't matter. Getting too close to this perky redhead was a bad idea, plain and simple. "My mom is making up my old room for you and Annie and the baby."

"Where will you sleep?"

"I claimed the couch."

"You okay with that?" Her eyes teased.

"No choice."

She gave him a wry smile. "In this huge house?"

He chuckled. "I'm not sleeping with my brothers."

Cam belched from the other room. And she laughed. "I see what you mean."

She didn't, though. No one did, except for maybe his mom. He didn't want to dream. And if he did, he'd be better off away from anyone who might hear. His mom had kept her promise and hadn't said a word to his dad. Andy Zelinsky wouldn't let something like that go if he knew, and Zach wasn't in the mood to talk about it. Not yet. He'd talked enough with the counselor on base once he'd returned stateside, *pink slip* and all. It hadn't done any good then, why would it now?

"Ginger, I placed some pj's, towels and a robe in your room." His mom briefly rubbed his back. "And Zach, there are blankets and a pillow and your pj's on the couch."

"Thanks, Mom." He still had clothes here. And considering the added company staying over, no doubt his mom wanted him decent. She didn't want him sleeping in his Skivvies.

"Yes, thank you, Helen." Ginger turned toward him after his mom left to check on the rest of the overnight guests. "Well, I guess I'll turn in."

He slammed his hands in his pockets before he touched that bouncy ponytail of hers. "We can see about making it to church in the morning."

"I already texted the worship leader, so no worries." She looked back up at him. "Good night."

"Good night." He watched her walk away with the sway of that red tail swishing between her shoulders.

She'd fit right in with his family. Of his six younger brothers and three sisters, only two were absent. His sister Cat and the youngest, Luke, who was away at college. The remaining siblings had kept Ginger busy, or maybe she'd been good at mingling. So much so, he'd barely spoken more than a few words to her throughout the evening.

He'd been aware of her, though. All too aware.

At dinner she had helped Annie and Matthew with the baby, holding that chunk of a kid so her friend could eat. After dessert, they'd stayed, hoping the weather might eventually clear, but it only grew worse. Ginger had played cribbage with his mom and two aunts. And then later still, she played pool in the basement with Cam and his sisters.

He and Darren had taken on the winning team of Cam and their baby sister, Erin, while Monica and Ginger looked on. Ginger had even added cheers and jeers along with the rest of them. As if she belonged here. In many ways, she fit in better than he did.

He entered the living room and threw another couple of logs on the fire.

"Nice girl." Cam sat in the recliner watching the local weather forecast on the eleven o'clock news. Blizzard warnings had been posted through the night until midmorning.

"Yeah." Zach changed into flannel pajama bottoms before slipping under a blanket he'd spread out on the couch. He adjusted the pillow, pulled the blanket over him and reached for a second cover.

"Mom says your shops are connected." Cam gave him a slanted grin.

"By a glass slider." At one time, it must have been one store.

"That's convenient."

"Yeah." Most of his immediate family had stopped in to see his studio, but Cam hadn't gotten around to it yet. "She's great with customers."

"I'm sure she is." Cam didn't hide the amusement in his voice.

"What's your point?"

"Point is that everyone loves your girlfriend."

"She's not my girlfriend." Zach answered too sharp.

"Right." Cam got up and tossed him the remote. "Welcome home."

"Yeah. You, too." Zach's younger brother was a professional sport fisherman, but he'd recently lost his biggest sponsor.

Cam snorted with contempt. "Not exactly my choice."

Zach knew how that felt. "Sorry, man."

Cam sighed. "Yeah. Me, too."

"G'night. And turn off that light."

Cam nodded and clicked the switch.

Zach shut off the TV and lay there watching the fire. Flames danced, casting shadows against the walls and onto the ceiling. The soothing sounds of snapping wood and the hiss and crackle of the fire finally lulled him into sleep…

He saw the flash in front, followed by an explosion that thundered through him, rattling the ground with a slam of pressure that stunned, and then a shower of dirt and rocks hit the hood. Rapid gunfire peppered metal, but it sounded muffled as if he wore earplugs.

He shook his head, trying to clear it.

Something ripped through the windshield of their vehicle. He felt it burn his arm, white hot and sharp, before he grabbed the wheel. The Humvee careened and he jerked away from the ball of flames that had been the lead truck and slammed into a ditch. Yelling orders to take cover and return fire, he wiped blood and bits of tissue from his eyes. The smell of burning fuel gagged him.

He opened the door and grabbed his sergeant, who'd been driving, but the guy slumped. Gone! Half of him gone.

"Zach!"

He jerked awake. Blinked a few times and stared at the pretty face in front of him. Soft red waves framed that face. And she held a baby.

"What?"

Ginger looked worried. No, she looked scared. Really scared. "Can you help me?"

He blinked again and sat up. "What?"

"Meet me in the kitchen." Then she quickly turned and dashed away.

Zach ran a hand through his hair. Had he been dreaming? Memories or nightmares, he couldn't always tell between the two. The smell of smoke was real, though. He inhaled the softer scent of wood smoke from smoldering embers. It wasn't the acrid black stuff from IEDs that burned like no other.

He shook his head to clear it. Sounds came from the kitchen, so he slipped off the couch and followed the noise. In the kitchen, Ginger was there. Her red hair looked gorgeously messy. A fussy baby was cradled awkwardly in her arms. "What are you doing?"

She wouldn't look him in the eyes, but she held the kid out. "Can you take him while I make a bottle?"

Zach looked at the boy but didn't reach for him. "Why are you doing this?"

"So Annie can get some sleep. He's still hungry and— Can you take him?"

He reached for the whiny little chunk before he cried outright and woke the entire house. "This kid's a load."

Ginger let loose a soft chuckle, but her movements seemed tense. "No, he's not." She stopped moving and openly stared at him. "Hey, you're not bad at that."

"What?" He rocked the little guy, who quieted down some.

"Holding babies." She gave him a once-over, but her eyes caught on the puckered mass of scar tissue on his left upper arm and stayed there. Finally, she asked, "Where'd you learn how?"

Zach shrugged. "Growing up, I had plenty of practice."

"That's right. You're the oldest of ten." Her voice sounded forced and way too cheerful—even for her.

"Six brothers and three sisters."

Ginger cocked her pretty head, but she seemed shaken. Nervous even. Baby or him? "Maybe you should be the one doing this then."

He gave her a nod. "Bring that bottle by the fire where it's warm."

"Be there in a sec." When she finally came into the family room, she handed him the bottle and looked more composed. "Want me to throw on another log?"

He settled into a rocking chair near the hearth and reached for the bottle. "Sure."

The baby latched on and slurped.

And Zach watched Ginger feed the flames. Her toenails were painted bright blue. Dressed in his mom's baggy flannel pj's with her face scrubbed clean, it didn't matter that she was old enough, she still looked too young.

Fresh-faced and innocent and probably sheltered, too. Yet she hadn't asked about his dream. Did she know? She had to.

Ginger sat at the end of the couch where he'd slept and tucked her bare feet under his blankets. "I'm surprised you don't have a family of your own."

An interesting way of asking why he wasn't married, or finding out if he'd ever been. "Never got around to it, I guess."

"How come?"

He gave her the truth. "I saw too many guys torn up over leaving their wives and kids. Having to shut down to do the job. I didn't want that juggle. And I didn't find anyone worth juggling." He checked the baby's progress. The bottle was nearly empty. "What about you?"

"What about me?"

"No boyfriends?"

She looked away. "Uh, no."

"How come?" He repeated her words.

She shrugged. "They're a hassle."

The baby sucked air.

"You better burp him." Ginger got up. "I'll get a towel."

Zach shifted the baby against his shoulder and gently patted until the deed was done along with a warm trail of spit-up.

"Whoops, too late." Ginger had returned brandishing a dampened dish towel. "Sit forward and I'll get it."

He settled the baby against his other arm, while she wiped off his shoulder.

Her fingers brushed his bare skin near the scar and she froze. "When did you get this?"

That raw whisper made him look into her wide brown eyes. "Three years ago."

She looked horrified, but pointed toward the knight tattoo on his other arm with the word ARMY across the shield. The one he'd taken heat for. "And that?"

"After I'd enlisted." As an enlisted man, getting tattooed with a crusading knight was unconscionable. Didn't matter that it was one fierce-looking armored dude, his tattoo resembled the West Point mascot too much and his company name not at all.

"What made you choose that one?" Even she knew enough to question it.

Zach shrugged. He'd been young and green and liked the idea of a knight on a noble quest. He'd been itching for a fight in those days, ready to conquer the world for good. But the reality of combat often twisted up good reasons until motives were a blank page of just following orders. "My dad went to West Point, so I grew up watching Army football. They're the Black Knights."

"Here, I better take him back." She gave him the towel and leaned down for the baby.

Her hair tickled his shoulder and he inhaled quick and sharp. She smelled nice. Really nice.

Like flowers and rain. He caught her wide eyes. Did she feel it, this hum of awareness between them? Like a couple of magnets lined up but drawn to move together and stick if they got close enough. Like now.

Ginger quickly stood. She held the baby's dark head close to hers like a shield, but then he saw her kiss the little guy's forehead. "Well, good night. And thanks for helping."

Zach nodded. "No problem."

She'd helped him, too, waking him before the worst of it. And she hadn't asked. He'd seen that look of fear in her eyes. She knew, but hadn't asked. He was grateful for that. He didn't want her to know the details. He couldn't expect her to understand how one wrong move had changed the lives of so many. His fault. He'd given the orders.

He didn't want to tell her. Not ever. He just wanted to forget.

Ginger woke with a start and sat up. Looking around, she noticed that Annie and the baby were gone, but their overnight bag remained. They were most likely downstairs, maybe even getting another bottle ready. Annie had been smart coming prepared to stay over. But then, with a baby, a mom had to be ready for anything.

An image of Zach thrashing on the couch flashed through her mind. The guy had nightmares and a gruesome scar to go with them. Three years ago, he'd said. What had happened that he dreamed of it still? Maybe it was best if she didn't know. If she didn't ask, she wouldn't be faced with what he'd had to do.

Tempted to remain under the warm covers, Ginger got up instead. She headed for the bathroom armed with a new toothbrush Helen said she kept by the dozens, just in case. Once in the hall, the sounds of conversation floated along with the smell of freshly made coffee and bacon. People were definitely up.

She tamped down the swishing unease in her stomach. It might be a long ride back to town with Zach this morning if she didn't face him and ask. But questions about his nightmare scratched like sandpaper. Rough and gritty. Did she even want to know the answers?

It explained so much. His contempt for her welcome-home parade and the discomfort he had when talking about his deployments. Whatever ate at the man's peace hadn't been dealt with. And Ginger knew all too well how old wounds festered into something rotten.

After she dressed and made it downstairs, Zach was the first person she made eye contact with as he leaned against the counter sipping coffee. He was dressed in yesterday's clothes, and his short hair looked as if he'd run his hands through it over and over. His bright blue eyes were sleepy. An image of his broad shoulders in an undershirt sneaked its way into her mind, too, unsettling her further.

He raised his mug toward her. "Roads haven't been plowed yet. Can't make it to your church."

Ginger nodded and peered out the windows. The wind had stopped blowing and even the sun shone brightly, but deep snowdrifts were everywhere. The family room's sliding glass door was half covered by white.

"Ginger." Helen touched her shoulder. "There's a pot of plain tea on the table with cream and sugar. Mugs are on the counter."

"Thank you. Is there anything I can help you with?" She scanned the table where Annie sat rocking John to sleep.

"Oh, no, everything's made and staying warm in the oven. Andy's plowing the driveway with a couple of the boys moving cars, but they'll be done soon. We'll eat after they come in."

Ginger glanced at Zach. How long would they be stuck here?

He moved toward her, empty mug in hand, and pulled out a chair for her at the table, near the teapot and Annie. "Might be a while."

Ginger took the offered mug and sat down. The table had fifteen place settings complete with juice glasses. She'd never seen so many matched plates before. Not in real life.

"Thanks again for feeding him last night," Annie said.

Ginger pointed. "He did."

Zach nodded.

"Thank you. I'm sorry he interrupted your sleep." Annie smiled.

"No problem." Zach sipped his coffee.

And Helen looked concerned but didn't say a word.

Annie saw that, too, and gave Ginger a want-details look.

She might be her best bud, but Ginger wasn't about to spill on Zach's nightmare. She didn't think he'd want that information out there. Pretending she didn't know might not be good, either, even though she wanted to feign ignorance.

Ignoring Zach's issues smacked way too much of her mother. Ginger wasn't about to bury her head in the proverbial sand, not if she might be of help. If Zach was open to help. In the meantime, she'd pray for him. He clearly needed it.

Male voices from the foyer announced that the driveway was clear.

"How's the road look?" Zach asked.

"Not yet plowed. We saw high drifts from the open field." Andy Zelinsky's cheeks were red. "No one's leaving yet."

Zach looked grim and sat next to her.

Monica had joined them at the table along with Zach's baby sister, Erin, and his brothers Cam, Matthew, Marcus and Benjamin. A couple of cousins, whose names Ginger couldn't remember, took their places, too. Darren hadn't stayed over. He had dogs to take care of and had braved the snowstorm. But Ginger had overheard that he'd made it home, after he'd called Helen.

Zach's mom carried covered pans to the table and then sat down, as well. "Let's pray."

Andy Zelinsky bowed his head and led his family in a prayer they recited in unison.

"Bless us, oh Lord, and these Thy gifts, which we are about to receive, from Thy bounty, through Christ, our Lord. Amen."

"Amen," Ginger whispered.

The pan covers were taken off to reveal heaps of bacon and steaming pancakes. And then there was a mad dash to fill plates while everyone chattered and passed butter and syrup and juice.

Ginger watched the action with awe. This was like something from an old TV show.

Laughter and teasing and warmth. A family this big and there'd been no yelling, no cursing or even slamming food on the table. No drama.

Matthew dished up a couple of pancakes for Annie and then traded it for the sleeping baby. Like a pro, he tucked John into his car seat and draped a blanket over his legs.

"Pancakes and bacon?" Zach held a plate in front of her.

"Thanks." She reached for it and her fingers brushed his. She glanced up. They shared a secret. One she really didn't want to know.

He stared back. "You look a little out of your element."

She looked away and slathered butter on her cakes, then doused them in warm syrup. "Totally."

"That's a nice change."

"Uh, why?" She leaned forward to bite into a forkful of dripping pancake.

"You can organize a whole town, but a simple family breakfast stops you cold."

"Amazed, I guess," she mumbled while syrup dribbled down her chin. "And there's nothing simple about it. These are awesome."

"My mom's a great cook." He narrowed his gaze. "But they're just pancakes. Surely you make pancakes."

Ginger looked away. A couple of frozen

waffles popped in the toaster were her Sunday morning treat or sometimes those cinnamon rolls from a tube. "Not like these."

Zach polished off his short stack in no time. He got up to refill his coffee and asked if anyone wanted more, as well. Watching him walk around the table, pot in hand, refilling mugs made her heart prick with envy.

Zach had a great family. A family that cared and was supportive. Loving.

Scanning the table, Ginger wondered how different her life might have been with a family like this one. There were no guarantees in life, but how one tackled problems was the proving ground for faith. God had helped her overcome her past, but that didn't mean she'd trust a man to provide a safe future.

Zach was the sort of man who invited trust with his long army career and budding new business. The gentle way he'd held little John proved he was a good man. But Ginger knew better than to allow the attraction she felt toward him to go any further. Dark resentments had twisted her father into a man who'd broken her heart over and over.

Ginger wasn't about to offer up her heart for Zach to do the same thing. He was a man with potentially serious issues of his own. Resentments and trauma might as well be interchangeable as far as she was concerned. The end result would always be the same. One way or another, Ginger was bound to get hurt.

Chapter Five

"Snowshoeing? I've never done it before, but I'm game to try." Ginger looked as eager to get out of the house as him.

"The sun is shining and there's no more wind. A perfect day."

Waiting for the secondary roads, such as the one his parents lived on, to be plowed was making Zach stir-crazy. He couldn't sit around any longer. A brisk walk with snowshoes would hopefully clear his mind of the list of things he'd hoped to get done today. The fact that a couple of his brothers and sisters were going as well made it okay to ask Ginger.

Ginger scrunched her nose. "Is it hard to do?"

"No."

"What about gear?"

His patience was definitely wearing thin. "We have everything. Come on."

She exchanged a look with Annie. That silent communication girlfriends were famous for. What they'd said with one look, Zach could only guess.

Ginger finally stood. "Okay, okay."

It didn't take long to slip into jackets, hats, mittens and boots. Ginger happened to be the same shoe size as his mom, so that made things easy. Those leather knee-high things she'd worn out here were useless.

"Ready?"

Ginger pulled a knit hat over her head. "As ready as I'll ever be."

He held the door for her. Once outside, he sat on the edge of the porch and showed Ginger how to get in and out of the snowshoe bindings. It was no surprise that his siblings hadn't waited for them. They were halfway across the backyard.

He stood and offered her his hand. "Now just walk."

She took a step and then another with no problems.

"See? Easy."

She laughed. "So far, but we haven't made it out of the yard." Once they got into deeper snow, Ginger tried to turn and teetered.

He reached for her hand. "I got you."

"Thanks. Backing up isn't so easy."

He chuckled. "Forward movement works best."

"With most things."

"True." He couldn't agree more, but sometimes the past had a way of moving forward, too, clinging like an ocean barnacle.

Many things Ginger said, or didn't say, nagged him. Her admission last night about no boyfriends was one of them. Why would a pretty girl like her have no boyfriends? And maybe more important, not want one?

They were in the open field now, their footfalls a rhythmic swooshing sound as they headed toward the woods. He pointed at the trunks marked with blue paint. "Those are the trees my dad will tap for syrup."

"That's a lot of trees."

Zach chuckled. "He makes a lot of syrup."

Her eyes widened as she looked around. "You know what? Maybe this would make a nice window display."

Zach looked, too. "What would?"

Ginger spread her arms. "The woods. I don't know, maybe some white birch branches with lights or some such."

"A bunch of sticks don't exude romance." He

gave her a wry grin. "Unless you're into that sort of thing."

She rolled her eyes. "No, you know, the sticks could be covered with spray snow to represent snow-covered trees. Globs of the white stuff whipped against the tree trunks look pretty when the sun hits. These woods shine like a crystal forest full of diamonds."

He didn't see it. "Diamonds aren't the theme."

"Diamonds are romance to some women." Ginger stopped walking and looked around again.

"Are you one of them?" He stopped, too.

Maybe that's why ordinary boyfriends held no interest. She wanted the big bucks, and there was a lot of it spread around the area come summertime. But then a tea and spice store wasn't exactly a rich-man magnet.

"You know, you're really good at insulting me." She glared.

The sun's rays caught the ends of her hair beneath the knit hat she wore, turning those thick curls to flame. The woman was pure fire even in the middle of a snowy forest of hardwoods.

The way she lifted her chin gave him the perfect angle to lean down and kiss her. It'd be so easy.

And another nightmare waiting to happen.

He raised his hands in surrender. "You're the one who said women like diamonds and crystal—"

She looked at him with challenge in her big brown eyes. "You're the artist. Don't you have a better idea?"

Than kissing her? "No."

"Then I guess it's no wonder you're paying me to do yours." She started walking, trudging one snow-shoed foot in front of the other.

"I'm paying so you'll wait on my customers," he corrected.

That wary look stole into her pretty eyes. "Why? I mean, you're the one who signed up for retail."

"Yeah, but you're better at it than me. The army doesn't teach soft customer service skills."

Her bright eyes dimmed. "How long were you in the service?"

"Nineteen years."

"Soooo, you joined when?"

"I enlisted right out of high school. My parents weren't thrilled. They wanted me to go to college first, do the ROTC thing, but I didn't want to be stuck sitting in a classroom for four years. I'd always wanted a military career, so I figured why wait?"

Ginger nodded. "So, you're a patient man."

"Right." He laughed, but then his stomach turned when Ginger's expression changed.

She looked far too thoughtful, and he knew what was coming by that tense look on her face. She was gathering her courage, choosing the right words. Then she took a deep breath and let it out. "You know, last night, you were having a pretty intense nightmare."

Not only did she call them what they were, but she'd seen it up close and personal. How badly had he thrashed and mumbled on that couch?

"Is that why you woke me?"

Again, Ginger stopped walking. Looking far too serious for someone so bubbly, she asked, "Do you have them often?"

"Here and there." He looked away. More so since coming back home.

Silence settled thick between them, but Ginger didn't move. She simply waited.

For what he wasn't sure, so he met her gaze. "What?"

She backed away and shook her head. "I'm sorry, it's none of my business."

That statement irritated him. "Sure it is. We both live and work in the same building. You've a right to worry whether I'll go postal."

Her eyes widened with real fear. "That's not what I meant."

"It should be." He wasn't an idiot. And getting to know this woman, he knew that neither was she. Last night, he'd scared her. Just as he scared her now. He let out a weary breath. "Ginger, it's okay. I'm working through it."

He meant that, even though he didn't want to talk about it with her or anyone else. He wanted to forget. He was trying to start over. What use was dredging up the past to someone not qualified to hear it? Not even close to understanding why he shouldn't be here. Good men with families had died, while he came home with a mere scratch.

They kept moving. But he could tell she wasn't comforted. If anything, she seemed even more tense than before.

They walked quite a ways without talking. The swooshing sounds of their movement blended with the bird calls surrounding them. Black-capped chickadees darted through the trees and nuthatches bounced up and down the tree trunks, yammering away. The path Zach followed through the woods eventually emptied out at the lake. He saw the tracks that crossed the lake, left by his brothers and sisters. They were probably already home.

Plowed roads or not, he wanted to pack up Ginger and get out of there. Get back to town and put some space between them. He took a few steps before he'd noticed that Ginger hadn't moved. She stayed put on the shoreline.

He pointed at the smattering of huts toward the middle. "It's frozen solid. See, there are ice fishermen out there safe and sound. And these tracks, they're fresh."

She didn't look convinced.

He'd never have taken her for a chicken over something so small as walking across a frozen lake. He gave her a grim smile. "Do you really think I'd let you walk on dangerous ground?"

Her big brown eyes grew bigger.

He held out his hand. "Come on, you can trust me."

After he said it, Zach realized the commitment that came with a statement like that. He'd made a pledge of honor. One he took seriously.

She looked him in the eyes for a long time. Searching his soul and weighing the imagined risks.

He waited. Hand still outstretched.

And then she placed her mitten-covered hand in his and something stirred deep inside.

He gave her a gentle squeeze. "You can do this, Ginger."

The drive back to Maple Springs couldn't have come at a better time. Ginger needed distance from Zach. Fortunately, while they'd been out snowshoeing, the county snowplows had gone through and opened the roads to town. Bundled up in the passenger seat, awfully close to the man she wanted to get away from, Ginger stared at the road ahead.

But the scent of outside clung to Zach's jacket. He smelled like frosty fresh air and sunshine, reminding her of their morning snowshoeing in the woods. And his help across that lake.

Only twenty minutes more and she could zone out and not think. She didn't want to think about this new connection with Zach.

"So, what happened there on the ice?" Zach's voice was soft. Gentle even.

Ginger briefly closed her eyes. Was it worse to let him think she had a nutty phobia or tell him why it had taken every ounce of willpower she had to walk across that frozen water while clutching his arm as if it were a safety harness?

She cleared her throat. "My little brother fell through the ice on a lake. I pulled him out, but then I'd coaxed him out there."

"How old were you?"

"Twelve. My brother was eight." Ginger would never forget the way her father had ripped her up one side and down the other. Lambasting her until her ears rang.

They came to a stop sign. With no one in

sight, Zach put the car in Park and faced her. His eyes were filled with real concern. "Was he okay?"

"He recovered, yes. But he lost the hearing in one ear because of an infection he'd caught in the hospital." And Ginger never forgot that kind of fear.

Fear of not getting her brother out of the water, and then the fear of him dying on the shore while she ran for help, followed by fear that he'd die in the hospital. Worst of all was that her father had never forgiven her. He'd turned that incident into a verbal weapon he'd used often enough for her to know.

"So, you're afraid to walk on frozen lakes."

"Lakes, ponds, rivers—that about covers all bodies of water." Ginger tried to make light of it.

Zach gave her half a smile as he drove forward. "You walked on one today."

Yes, she had. After refusing to follow Zach, she'd finally given in. How come? He'd assured her that where they'd tread wasn't over deep water. Not once had he said her fear was silly or stupid. Not once had he barked at her for moving so slow or gripping his arm too tight. This impatient man had been patient with her.

She stared at him. "Thanks."

He looked at her. "No problem. I got your back."

Ginger wanted to believe him.

She had no reason not to. Zach Zelinsky seemed to be a man of his word. An honest man with fears of his own. Fears he battled in nightmare form. Today, she'd walked across an icy lake despite her fears. With Zach's help. Could she repay him the favor?

His flippant comment about going postal hinted that his issues ran deeper than a frozen-water phobia. He'd said he was working through it. What did that mean? How was he doing that? And could she even ask?

He'd asked her to trust him, but that was a tough one. Her father had broken her heart over and over with his cruel put-downs and resentments. She couldn't trust her own family to be there when she needed them. Why would Zach be any different?

Monday Ginger spent half her day off on a wholesale tea-and-spice-buying trip in Traverse City. The weather had cooperated with clear skies and cold winter sunshine. She only wished her bank account wasn't nearly as frozen. She'd purchased only enough inventory for the upcoming Valentine's Day push.

After one taste, she chose an expensive cinnamon-clove chai complete with rose petals as the tea blend to inspire romance. It smelled amazing, inspiring thoughts of mystery and falling in love. Even better, it looked pretty, too.

She entered the back of her shop with a huge brown shopping bag and heard the deep drumbeat of rock music coming from next door. Her pulse picked up speed.

Zach was in his studio.

Setting her bag down, she tossed around the idea of seeing what he was up to. Should she? Shouldn't she? She finally gave up and stepped through her shop. Spotting a couple of women peering through Zach's window, Ginger hesitated. When they didn't leave after a few more moments, she unlatched the slider and gave it a tug. Zach rarely locked his side, so she walked right in and gave the ladies a wave.

They waved back and pointed.

Really curious, Ginger stepped farther into Zach's studio. Songs she didn't recognize blared from a small speaker on the counter, near Zach's phone. The same one he used to swipe credit cards.

He sat at the workbench. With one hand, he rolled a long metal pipe. His other hand cradled a glowing blob of molten glass at the pipe's end with wet newspaper, causing steam to circle around him.

What struck her was the deep concentration

on his face. And the joy she read there. Mesmerized like the ladies out front, Ginger didn't interrupt. She simply watched him shape, clip and then stick that pipe with the molten mass of glass back in the furnace, only to repeat the cycle again. And again.

He'd noticed her, gave her a quick nod, but didn't stop. Probably couldn't.

This was why he wanted her help in waiting on his customers. He couldn't do this and wait on customers, too. He'd had a lot of traffic when he'd first opened. Would that taper off now that folks knew he was here? Ginger glanced at Zach's storefront window, where a few more had joined the audience.

Probably not.

Zach stood again. A masculine sight in jeans and a sweat-dampened T-shirt. That awful-looking, puckered scar on his left arm taunted her as he moved. Were his dreams about that injury or something else?

She didn't know how long she watched him and didn't care. The process was fascinating. When Zach finally tapped that long metal pole and the elegantly fluted glass vase with swirls of color fell off onto a fortified table, she heard the sound of muffled applause coming from outside. She wanted to clap, too.

Zach gave his audience a quick wave and

donned a pair of what looked like long heavy-duty oven mitts. He lifted the vase, walked it over to what he'd called an annealer and set it deep inside. After closing the doors, he slid the mitts off and wiped his brow, then turned down the music. "Hey."

Ginger glanced at the window. "Looks like your spectators are leaving."

"Yeah." Zach's brow furrowed.

"You had quite the audience out there."

He shrugged. "It's a neat thing to watch."

Not to mention the man, but Ginger wasn't going to admit that. Not out loud, anyway. "It was really cool. So now what?"

"Now? I'm hungry and I'm going to grab a sandwich at the place across the street. Want anything?" He slipped on a sweatshirt and then his jacket.

Bernelli's was her favorite. And she hadn't eaten since breakfast. Ginger made a move toward her shop. "Let me get my wallet."

Zach waved her off. "I got it. Tell me what you want."

Ginger hesitated.

He cocked one eyebrow at her indecision.

"Okay, fine. I'll take a chicken avocado club."

He gave her a nod and left.

Well, the impatient Zach Zelinsky was back in full force.

Ginger returned to her shop, leaving the glass slider between their stores open, and put away her purchases. It didn't take long.

Coming back out front, she stared at her storefront window. The heart-shaped teapots she'd ordered should be in soon. They'd look nice incorporated into her display somehow. Whatever that display might be. With Valentine's Day only three weeks away, she needed to decide pretty soon. With Zach's offer, she could afford decorations, but they needed to be up when the voting tab on the chamber's website went live in two weeks. The community had five full days to cast their votes for the best window. Ginger wanted those votes.

What was it about Maple Springs that enticed lovers? How could she get that theme across while promoting her tea and Zach's glasswork so that both windows tied together somehow?

"I got you an iced tea."

Zach's voice startled her and she whipped around. "I didn't hear you come in."

He shrugged and headed for her back room. "Want to eat in here?"

"Sure." Ginger followed, her stomach growling. She hadn't expected they'd eat together, but then, why not? They were both here, working. On their day off. How pathetic.

Zach pulled out two foil-wrapped sandwiches, a couple of bags of chips and cookies while Ginger set her small table with paper plates and napkins.

Sliding into a chair opposite, she waited for Zach to sit down, too, but he was looking over her newly stocked shelves. "I went shopping."

"I see that, but you didn't buy much." He looked too intently at her rather bare shelves.

She shrugged. She couldn't afford much, but she wouldn't admit that aloud, either. "I picked up a really nice Valentine's Day chai tea blend. Besides, I like my tea leaves fresh, so I don't buy too much in bulk."

He finally sat down. "You didn't have to wait for me."

"I wasn't sure if you'd pray over the food."

He gave her a crooked half grin. "Go ahead."

"Maybe you could say your family's dinnertime prayer?" She didn't want to pray aloud in front of him. That seemed too personal and sort of intimate.

He bowed his head and quickly said the words she barely remembered but had liked the sound of. They had a nice rhythm and sweet appreciation and could be recited without baring one's soul.

When he'd finished, he handed her the bottle of unsweetened iced tea. What a guy.

"Thanks for getting this." She shook the bottle before opening it. "And you remembered no sugar."

"Not that hard to do. So, you really like tea?" He bit into his sandwich.

Ginger squashed the butterflies in her belly. She really shouldn't read into his words but couldn't help it. Zach remembered stuff about her. "Uh, yeah. Why?"

He shrugged. "Just trying to figure out how you got here, doing this."

"I started working for Sally while I attended the community college up here. This whole space was once her pottery shop along with tea and spices. I eventually took over the tea and spice part of the store and one thing led to another and now I own it. So here I am."

"Here you are." He saw straight through her and looked as if he might be disappointed. He leaned back in the chair and wiped his mouth with a napkin. "Did you always want to have a tea store?"

She looked away. "Not necessarily tea, not even a store per se, but I've always wanted to run my own business."

"And why's that?"

She laughed. "Be my own boss. You know, take orders from no one but me."

He looked thoughtful.

"So, what's with all the questions?"

"Just making conversation."

Of course he didn't care. Not really. They were making small talk while they ate, because they were neighbors. Friendly neighbors. That's the way it should be. And if she was smart, that's all they'd ever be.

Chapter Six

A couple of days later, while Ginger waited on Zach's customers, she spotted Annie entering through the slider door from her shop. Giving her friend a nod, she cleared through the short line of women buying glass hearts and multicolored globes.

It didn't take long.

"Wow." Annie took in the small group of women watching Zach at work with molten glass.

Ginger rolled her eyes. "I know."

"What is all this?"

Ginger lowered her voice. "His fan club. Some of these ladies come every morning."

"You're kidding." Annie chuckled.

"I'm not." Ginger chuckled. She didn't know what she envied more—that he had customer fans or that she was too busy to join them.

There were a range of ages, but the daily ones were a few older ladies who stopped in after they'd met for breakfast at the diner around the corner. One of the women wrote for the *Maple Springs Gazette*, circulation—not many, and she wanted to do a spread on Zach.

Zach had laughed but grudgingly agreed under the condition that she stayed focused on his work with glass and the shop. What he didn't say, Ginger had heard loud and clear. His war experience and military career were off-limits for questions. Maybe even for her, too.

"Looking for tea?" Ginger gestured toward her own counter.

"That and stopping in to say hello before I head to my dance class. Marie is watching the baby." Annie walked with her through the glass slider. "So…how come you're waiting on Zach's customers?"

"We made a deal."

"And?" Annie's eyebrows rose.

Ginger didn't make a big deal about it. "I watch his shop while he does hot glasswork and he'll pay for the window display supplies."

"Nice." Annie poured herself a sample cup of the romantic chai blend. "Mmm, this is good. I'll buy a bag, please. Have you decided on your window then?"

"No. I need to get moving on it, but I'm at a loss."

"You always do a nice display, so what's the trouble?"

Ginger shrugged. She didn't want to give voice to her fears that she wasn't creative enough to pull this one off. She'd never won a window display contest before.

She sighed instead. "Brady wants an update on how many merchants have committed to participating. He'll remind everyone tonight at the meeting, but it's up to me to follow up and push, you know? Make sure everyone's in. And I need to be upbeat about it, too."

"Your usual self, then." Annie took another sip of tea. "So I take it you're going."

Ginger didn't miss a meeting, but she didn't feel so positive about this one. "Yes, I'm going. Are you?"

"I hate to leave John." Annie loved her baby to pieces.

That was to be expected in a new mom, sure, but Ginger knew the grief her friend had been through trying to get pregnant, and then the pain of losing her husband plus the added turmoil over falling for Matthew so quickly afterward. Annie kept a low profile these days.

Ginger scooped aromatic loose tea into a

plastic bag. "If I had that little man waiting for me at home, I wouldn't go, either."

"Go where?" Zach stood in the doorway, appearing from out of nowhere.

Annie waved hello while she sipped her tea.

"Hey, Annie." He gave her a nod.

"The chamber meeting," Ginger told him.

"Oh." The tone of his voice sounded preoccupied, but his eyes glowed with satisfaction and something close to joy.

No doubt he looked pleased from having created something special out of a clump of hot glass. It was no wonder he drew an audience. Especially female. Today, he'd seemed okay with it. The day before, those feminine titters and stares had irritated him to no end.

"It's the one with the really good food." Ginger handed over the bag and waved away Annie's attempt to pay. "It's on me."

"You really should check it out, Zach," Annie added. "You might be able to protect Ginger from the book-man's unwanted advances."

"Annie!" Ginger wanted to crawl under her counter and hide.

Zach's eyes narrowed. "Who's the book-man?"

Knowing her face was on fire, Ginger cringed. "He works at the library."

"And he's been after Ginger for a date ever

since they attended a chamber-sponsored class together." Annie gave her a wink.

Ginger glared. "I have nothing to worry about with Lewis."

"Hmm." Annie glanced at her watch. "Oops, I gotta run. 'Bye."

They both watched her exit.

"Is she serious about this guy bothering you?"

"No. Well, it's not a big deal. We worked on a project for that class, and well, he can't seem to take the hint that I'm not interested." Ginger wouldn't want to run into Lewis in a dark alley—not because he was dangerous; he wasn't. He was simply a little odd and clung like lint.

Zach rubbed his chin.

Ginger changed the subject fast. "Hey, I have an idea for the windows. What do you think about big puffy cotton clouds raining teapots in my window and glass globes in yours?"

"How's that romantic?"

Zach had asked the question innocently enough, but an image of him caught in the rain had her skin tingling. "Um…I don't know. Nice things for a rainy day?"

"You can do better."

"Like what?"

His eyes narrowed. "Dig deeper."

"Right." He was no help. No help at all. No brainstorming of ideas. Nothing. "Deeper into what?"

He raised one eyebrow at her, as if she was pretty dense for not understanding where to dig for romance.

Ginger raised her chin. She didn't bare her soul to anyone. She certainly couldn't do it for a window display. How dismal would her heart look represented by her window? It'd be like something from a sporting goods store with layers of padded protection.

He turned to leave.

"Wait." Ginger came out from around her counter. "What's the spending limit here?"

"What's your time worth?"

Ginger cocked her head. "What do you mean?"

"Multiply your hourly rate by the hours you cover my store and put into the displays. There's your budget."

She stared at him. "My hourly rate?"

He cocked one infuriating eyebrow again. "How much is an hour of your time worth in dollars and cents?"

"I don't know." Ginger huffed. "What's a fair price?"

"Only you know that."

Ginger opened her mouth, but then stopped

and thought about it. What was her time worth? "I'll have to get back to you."

He gave her that crooked lift of his lips that was barely a smile and walked back to his shop. Frustrating man. But he'd made a point. A good one.

Ginger had sunk countless hours into her store and the community hoping to increase business, hoping that if folks liked what they saw in her, they'd buy what she sold. Never once had she considered the cost of her own time, her *hourly rate*. Did she even clear minimum wage? Surely, the satisfaction of a job well done along with the appreciation from others counted for something.

She liked to tell herself that much of what she did was to grow her business. It wasn't about acceptance. It wasn't about proving herself worthy of respect. But she knew better. She lapped up the approval given by others like a thirsty Great Dane. She wanted to be somebody. And in Maple Springs, she was. People knew her and for the most part, they cared.

In spite of the new coffee shop stepping on her toes, Ginger wasn't a quitter. Not anymore. She'd work harder, and getting her business name out there statewide would no doubt help.

If she won the window display contest.

She had to win. Failure wasn't an option, because it couldn't be. If she let those thoughts in with all the doubt that came with it, she'd be doomed before she started.

Dig deeper...

She glanced at Zach. He was sort of the pot calling the kettle black with that statement. Wasn't he?

All those years of hearing her father say she wouldn't amount to anything special had stayed with her. It drove her. The scary part was what if she dug deep and it still wasn't enough? It'd be as if those words she'd heard her whole life were true.

That evening, Zach quickly showered and dressed in a pair of jeans, turtleneck and a sweater. He didn't think anyone expected a suit even though the restaurant sponsoring the chamber meeting was on the high side of uppity.

He was going because of Ginger.

And that gnawed at him. He didn't do these things, didn't care about chumming with the local dignitaries and business owners. He didn't like crowds or crowded places. He wanted to make stuff with glass, sell it and be left alone. Zach knew what his time was worth, and the Maple Springs Chamber of Commerce couldn't afford him. Maybe no one could.

But the thought of big brown eyes made worried over some creep badgering her was another matter. One he couldn't let go. He'd told Ginger she could trust him to keep her safe, and that's what he was doing. He'd check this guy out for himself before believing Ginger's admission that it was no big deal.

He slipped on his coat and headed out. It wasn't far. A couple of blocks' walk at most. Another reason to go. It wouldn't take long to get in, check things out and then exit.

After snowshoeing with Ginger on Sunday, Zach realized there was more to the bubbly personality than he first thought. There were things about her that bothered him. No boyfriends. No mention of family, other than the little brother who'd fallen through the ice.

She seemed completely alone in Maple Springs. Monica said that Ginger spread herself thin considering everything she did. Known and loved by everyone, yet who'd she hang out with other than Annie Marshall? Who had Ginger's back?

He stepped into the foyer of a tiny upscale restaurant with its deep wood tones and rich-looking upholstered chairs. It was crammed tight with people hanging up coats and moving inside.

The itchy feeling of being boxed in scratched through him. Taking deep breaths, he scanned the walls for another exit and noticed one through the doorway leading into the dining area, on the other side of the bar.

Okay, okay. He had another way out if needed.

Looking down, Zach spotted an ornate woven rug on the wood floor. The same kind of rug he'd seen in an Afghan village. In the blink of an eye, he was back there, on patrol with his men, looking for insurgents. Men and women spoke quickly in a language he didn't understand. Their gestures he knew, though, a mix of anger and fear as he and his men went door-to-door. A dog barked in the distance.

After taking fire, they'd kicked in the door to a place with a rug like this one, with woven threads of gold and brown in an intricate pattern. A thing of beauty in an ugly place.

A shriek of laughter echoed through his ears, startling him, pulling him back to the present. He felt a guy grab his collar and jerked back to loosen the hold.

But the guy pulled him toward the doorway. "Zach Zelinsky. I heard you'd moved back home. How are you?"

He'd made a fist and was ready to throw it when he blinked instead, recognizing a pair of wide eyes he remembered from high school. "Charlie?"

Charlie let go and backed up, nervously running a hand through his thinning hair. "Wow. Look at you. Still mean and lean. I heard you retired from the army."

"Yeah. Sorry." Zach felt like an idiot.

"What are you doing now?"

Zach relaxed. Sort of. Adrenaline still pumped through his veins. He'd reacted too quick and had nearly clocked someone. "Opened a glass shop on Main."

Charlie tipped his head back in shock. "The artsy one?"

"The same."

His old school friend whistled. "My wife was in there the other day and said it's pretty cool. Have you got your insurance lined up? If you need anything, let me know." Charlie slipped him a business card. "I'm an independent agent, so I can hook you up with the best deal." Then he gave him a nod. "Gotta run. Big client over there."

"No problem." And so it went. Charlie was all about networking now. Scoring the next contact that might make him money. That's what these things were for. And Zach wanted no part of it.

"I didn't think you'd come." Ginger walked up to him, smiling and beautiful.

He shrugged. "So, where's this dude?"

"Who?"

He searched his memory for the guy's name. "Lewis?"

Ginger gritted her teeth. "I'm going to kill Annie. Seriously, that's why you came, to play protector or something equally stupid?"

Trained to protect. What did she expect? "It got me here."

"I suppose that's one way of looking it at." Her hair fell in lush red waves around her shoulders. She wore the same black pants and sweater that she had on earlier along with a pair of boots that had ridiculously high heels.

Zach mused that he could look at her all night. Look, but don't touch. Playing protector might have its advantages. He leaned toward her. "Where is he?"

"I haven't seen him." Ginger gave him a smug smile and wandered away. Not far, though. The crowd was too thick.

Zach made his way toward the bar. He could see the entire place from there, and if he turned around, he'd see everything through the mirror on the wall behind shelves of expensive liquor bottles.

He ordered a pop, leaned back against the bar of carved mahogany and watched people. Folks with drinks in hand, making small talk about nothing, wasting time. His sister Monica came to these kinds of things, but he didn't see her tonight and he didn't recognize most of the people present, either. He wouldn't have known Charlie if he hadn't approached Zach first. Twenty years away from a place had a way of making things unfamiliar.

A waitress came around with a tray of funky-looking snacks and offered him one. He wasn't sure what it was, but it tasted good so he grabbed another two before she left.

Searching the restaurant, he spotted Ginger. She'd made it across the room and chatted comfortably with a group of older women. The sound of her laughter was warm and infectious. He heard it from where he stood.

A strong, powdery scent tickled his nose.

"I sure hope Ginger and her tea shop make it."

Zach looked down at an old lady. Definitely wearing lilac-scented something, she stood next to him and she wasn't talking to anyone else that he could tell. "Ma'am?"

"It's where I buy my tea and always have. Be a shame to see her fold."

"Why would she?" Zach probed.

The old lady shrugged. "Retail is tough. Stands to reason when that new coffee shop started selling loose tea, Ginger faced competition. But it's a messy place. Those kids with their ratty hair and tattoos."

Zach chuckled. He'd have loved to hear what this lady might say about his tattoo. But then the wicked knight was tame compared with some of the coffeehouse-grunge ink. He didn't care what they looked like as long as the service and coffee were good. Both were very good, and the place was always busy.

"Ginger's such a sweet girl."

Why was she telling him this?

The old lady winked at him. "And single, too."

"So I've heard." Zach extended his hand. "Zach Zelinsky."

She gave him a firm handshake and didn't let go. "I know who you are."

He tipped his head. "You have me at an advantage, ma'am."

"Sally Monroe."

"Ahh, you're the woman I bought the building from." He'd never met her because even though he'd toured the building when he'd been home for Darren's wedding, he'd gone after hours with her real estate agent. Due to his short leave, he'd had to sign all the closing paperwork through the mail.

There was something warm and caring about Sally's honest gaze that reminded Zach of his mother. This small gray-haired woman who smelled like lilacs saw a lot.

She finally let go of his hand, but her gaze held on. "You've made nice changes to the shop. I peeked in the window."

"Thank you." He tipped his head, ready to invite her to stop in for a tour, but heard Ginger's approach. It had to be her high-heeled boots clicking quickly on the hardwood floors.

"Sally!" Ginger gave the woman a big hug. "I didn't know you were in town. Why didn't you call?"

"I arrived this afternoon and thought I'd come by tonight and surprise you." Sally looked at Zach. "We attended many of these functions together."

He nodded.

"She taught me everything. Way better than school. Have you met Zach?" Ginger gave the woman's shoulders a quick squeeze before letting go.

"Yes, just now. And a fine young man." Sally patted his arm.

He was neither.

Ginger gave him a long, thoughtful look. Maybe she agreed with her mentor. But then she turned toward Sally. "How long are you staying?"

"Just today and tomorrow."

"Have you had dinner? We could go out—"

Sally tapped her arm. "I've already eaten at June's. I'm staying there tonight, but thank you."

Ginger stuck her lip out in a pout before adding, "You have to come by the shop."

"I will." Sally nodded and then gave him a stern look. "Tomorrow, when you open."

Zach looked forward to showing the old lady all the changes he'd made. How did she know him if she didn't live here anymore? Or was the reason Sally approached him because she'd caught him admiring Ginger from afar? She seemed pleased by that, but with reservation.

Zach had his own reservations, but Sally obviously cared. Maybe seeing the shop had more to do with how he'd treat Ginger than anything else. He didn't want to let either of them down.

The chamber of commerce president quieted the crowd for a short business meeting. The guy mentioned ZZ Glassworks as a newly opened shop, thanked him for coming and then asked if Ginger had signed him up for membership.

"Not yet," Zach said.

"Don't worry, she will." The chamber president sounded confident. And the crowd laughed as expected.

He caught Ginger's gaze, and she smiled.

Zach steered his attention back to the chamber president as he launched into the upcoming town events to celebrate Valentine's Day, including a swing band playing two weekends in a row at the Maple Springs Inn's outdoor pavilion. The window display contest information came next, and Brady announced that Ginger would be the one to contact with any questions.

Spread too thin.

Ginger elbowed him in the ribs and whispered, "That's Brady Wilson, the chamber president. I'll introduce you later, if you want."

He leaned close to her ear. "I don't want."

She shook her head as if he was a lost cause.

Zach glanced at Sally Monroe.

The old lady gave him an encouraging smile.

If Sally wanted to play matchmaker, she scouted out the wrong guy in him. Especially for someone as sunny as Ginger.

But he hadn't seen anyone who might be good enough for her, either. One more glance, and he spotted a short, skinny guy with thick glasses inching his way toward Ginger. Was that the book-man? He looked harmless enough but kept glancing at Ginger with hope in his eyes.

Zach moved closer to her and whispered, "To your left, is that him?"

Ginger gave him a quick nod. Then she waved at the guy.

Lewis, the book-man, waved back. But one look at Zach and the guy's smile froze until it dipped down with disappointment.

Zach didn't perceive a threat from the guy, and their message had been received. It wouldn't hurt to give this book-man a stronger message that read: Ginger is spoken for.

Zach slipped his arm around her waist and pulled her closer, whispering in her ear, "Okay, he's harmless."

"I told—" she turned her head faster than he'd leaned back and they touched noses "—you..."

He searched her gaze with longing. He wanted what little distance there was between them to disappear, but didn't make a move. This certainly wasn't the place, but then again, he'd wanted to send a stronger message. He slid his hands to her hips and smiled, daring her to do something in return.

Ginger's eyes widened and then narrowed as if trying to figure out what to do with him standing so close.

Applause from the crowd erupted, startling them both. Ending the moment.

He hadn't backed away. "What now?"

"Now we leave." Her voice sounded unusually raspy.

The crowd pushed forward, bumping Ginger into him. For once he didn't mind being penned in and cradled her close. "Looks like we're stuck."

Her hands pushed against his chest. "It'll let up soon. Where's Sally?"

He craned his neck and spotted the old lady weaving her way through like a pro. "She's halfway to the door."

"She'll be by in the morning." Ginger wiggled away and turned her back to him.

He spotted Lewis heading for them, against the tide of people, jamming everyone up. They weren't going anywhere anytime soon. For once, he didn't care.

Someone bumped her shoulder hard, sending her straight back into Zach. Again. She felt his hands grip her elbows. At least she wasn't facing him. For a minute there, she thought he'd—well, maybe she'd imagined that intent look in his eyes.

Ginger hadn't imagined her reckless response, though. Crazy as it was, she'd wanted to kiss him. Right here in the middle of a crowded room.

She spotted Sally at the door. The woman turned and waved. She'd made it out just fine, but then she was a slight woman with years of practice at this sort of thing. Having been an active volunteer in the community for aeons, Sally was a pro at bobbing and weaving through a chamber meeting crowd.

"She's pretty spry." Zach's deep voice rumbled through her back.

"Yeah." Ginger was practically smashed against him. Aware of every move Zach made behind her, aware of the heat from the palm of his hand resting on the small of her back as he steered her forward. All too aware of him.

Too many people tried to leave at once. Those staying for dinner made their way against the crowd toward the dozen or so tables covered with white linen cloths. The place was small anyway and there was nothing to do but wait their turn to leave.

"Hello, Ginger." Lewis blocked her path.

She stopped and Zach bumped into her. This time, his hands went around her waist again, and the scoundrel rested his chin on her shoulder as if it belonged there.

"Oh. Hi, Lewis. Hey, I'd like you to meet a friend of mine. This is Captain Zach Zelinsky."

Lewis pushed his glasses up the bridge of his nose. "You're that guy from the parade."

Zach possessively pulled her closer as he extended one hand toward the book-man. "Lewis."

Ginger held her breath. Would this work?

Would Zach's little show finally clue Lewis in that she wasn't interested?

"Welcome back to the area." Lewis took Zach's hand for a brief shake and gave him a thorough scan up and down. "Thank you for your service."

"Honored. And it's good to be back. Stop by the store sometime." Zach sounded genuinely warm and welcoming.

"Yeah, maybe." Lewis nodded and, with slumped shoulders, let them both pass without a backward glance.

Ginger released her breath in a whoosh. It had worked. She pressed forward, away from Zach. Grabbing her coat, she made it out the door into the cold night air. She quickly pulled out a scarf from the sleeve, wound it around her neck and slipped into her coat but didn't bother buttoning it up. She was still overheated.

Zach followed her, zipping up his jacket and ramming his hands in the pockets. His breath blew white in front of him.

"Thank you for, ah, the Lewis thing back there."

"You said playing protector was stupid." He glanced at her.

"Yeah, well, I was wrong." Ginger pulled on her fuzzy mittens. "I think he got the message."

"Good."

Why'd he look so angry about it? "And thanks for coming tonight. See, it wasn't so bad."

"Hmmph." Zach kept walking. Fast.

Ginger had trouble keeping up. "Can you slow down a little?"

He stopped all right, abruptly, and growled, "It's those heels."

"Maybe so, but the polite thing would be to offer your arm."

He let loose a bark of laughter. "The smart thing would be to wear decent winter boots."

"Are you questioning my intelligence?" She grabbed his arm anyway.

He leered at her. "If the boot fits…"

She mock punched his shoulder. "You're really a jerk."

He laughed again and looped her hand around the crook of his elbow. "Tell me something I don't know."

"You have quite the group of fans." She grinned.

"What are you talking about?"

She teased more. "You've got yourself real live groupies, Zach."

"They're old. I don't think that counts."

"Not all of them. Maybe I should decorate your window in glitz and glam, like you're a rock star, huh?"

"Do that, and I'll raise your rent."

Ginger stopped and pulled away from him, irrationally irritated that their little show was over. It wasn't real. "While we're on the subject—you know, sending me that letter about your rent increase was really lame."

"What'd you want me to do?"

"Pick up the phone."

He shrugged. "Why? I gave you all the information."

She couldn't believe he didn't get it. "Common courtesy? You could have introduced yourself."

"I did. At the parade, I came looking for you."

"To point out it was all nonsense." Ginger huffed.

"Yeah, well, I had better things to do than walk around on display."

Ginger clenched her teeth. That meant a lot to this town, a chance to show some appreciation. Surely he could give Maple Springs that opportunity without complaining. "Evidently your time's worth more than mine."

He looked really irritated now. "Time's not something to fritter away."

And she did? "Is that why you're paying for the windows? Do you think it's beneath your brilliance to bother giving me some ideas? Everything I've suggested—"

He moved fast.

Zach grabbed the lapel of her open coat and pulled her against him. In the glow of the streetlamps above, she could see that he had a wild look in his eyes as he searched hers. Like a man harassed for the last time.

Before she could speak, let alone stop her heart from racing, he kissed her.

Hard.

She gripped his forearms, but wearing mittens, she couldn't hold on well. She could barely stand upright, either, and swayed right into him. With her head spinning and heart pounding like crashing waves against a breakwall, she knew her knees would give out next and then she'd drop to the icy sidewalk.

Then what?

He'd probably leave her sitting there like an idiot.

Fire shot through her veins and she decided to kiss him back. Just to see…

His lips softened for a mere second or two but then he ended it. He pulled back quickly as if maybe he'd changed his mind.

Just when things were getting interesting!

"Whhaaatttt! W-why'd you d-do that?"

He grinned at her teeth-chattering stutter. A furiously pleased-with-himself kind of grin. "To shut you up."

"Ooh, that's it. You're…" Ginger reared back and let one arm swing. She'd slap that silly smirk off his face.

Zach caught her wrist and chuckled. "Careful."

She stared at him.

He stared back.

And he looked amused, full of regret, and maybe even a hint of disgust lay mixed in the myriad of emotions darkening his blue, blue eyes.

Ginger was disgusted, too. She couldn't decide what she wanted more—to hit him really hard or kiss him again.

Chapter Seven

Zach looked into Ginger's blazing eyes and knew he'd crossed the line. He let go of her wrist. It took everything he had to step back when he wanted nothing more than to pull her close and kiss her again. Slow this time and more thoroughly.

He couldn't stay numb around Ginger. She was flaring emotion and in-your-face feelings—all the stuff he feared. If he let himself feel, it'd all come back. And all those raw emotions unleashed would ruin him. Ruin her, too, if she got close enough.

He couldn't let that happen.

"Come on, it's cold out here." He slammed his hands deep into his coat pockets and headed for home. He didn't offer his arm, as touching Ginger couldn't end well, so he kept his distance. But he'd slowed down.

She walked next to him, her coat still open to the frigid air, completely silent.

He'd shut her up all right.

When they reached the back of his building, Zach opened the door for her.

She looked at him. "Thanks for walking me home."

He nodded, feeling lower than dirt.

Before he could say anything, apologize even, Ginger ran up the stairs and disappeared into her apartment with a slam of her door.

Zach sighed. He owed her an apology. Instead, he made his way to his own apartment. Shedding his coat, he looked at his place with the brown leather couch and chair. His weight bench sat in the corner and the wooden mini-blinds were drawn shut against the streetlights shining in from Main Street. His apartment was devoid of color. And feeling.

This is who he'd become.

He entered his tiny kitchen and made a sandwich.

Clicking on the TV, he tried to shut out what had happened with Ginger. He didn't want to care for her, but knew how easy it'd be to do just that. Everything about her was vibrant and warm and full of life. She drew out those dead parts of him and teased him with promises of maybe. As if maybe they could be something. Maybe she was what he needed.

Maybe…

After eating, he stared at the TV without watching it. He finally turned it off, got up and changed into an old T-shirt. He might as well get some work done and burn off this itchy restlessness.

He stepped out of his apartment at the same time Ginger came out of hers. She was dressed in running gear.

"Kinda late for a run." His voice came out in a low growl.

She raised her chin. "I won't feel like going in the morning, not that I need your permission."

"No. You don't." Would she stay inside if he asked her not to go?

She'd become his concern and he wanted to protect her. He'd protect her from herself if he had to, and he didn't like it that she seemed restless, too. He didn't know whether to be flattered or furious that he'd driven her to seek out running at nine o'clock at night. This was Maple Springs—a small town where running at night would be fine. She'd be fine, but still.

Ginger anchored the earbuds of her phone and passed by him. She flew down the stairs without once looking back.

Zach headed for his shop. The molten glass was hot and waiting for him to make something. He'd make anything to keep his thoughts at bay.

Once inside his workshop, he turned up the temperature of the smaller glory hole furnace and prepped the area. He was in the mood to make globes filled with twisted strands of glass. They had a pagan history, but he didn't worry about that. God was bigger than any superstition. Zach didn't name them; he simply made them for their beauty. And tonight, they perfectly suited his messed-up mood.

Ginger ran hard, but thoughts of Zach and that kiss stayed with her. Like a blister, it swelled and hurt and pretty much made her miserable no matter how far or fast she ran.

Did she really want to get involved with a guy so twisted up inside that he had nightmares? It didn't matter that he had more than a legitimate reason for them. Zach was grouchy as her father had been. And her father had nearly crushed her with his careless words and venomous moods.

When she finally made it home, she leaned against the back door, trying to catch her breath. She could hear Zach in his workshop with that heavy rock music playing. At close to ten o'clock, he was wise not to blast the volume as he had before.

She heard a masculine yelp, followed by a crash. And then silence.

Was he hurt?

An image of him cut and bleeding flashed through her mind and made her feet move before she thought it through. The back door to his shop was open, so she pushed on it.

It was hot inside. And she might be jumping from the frying pan right into the fire, but Ginger walked in anyway. "Zach?"

"Yeah?"

She kept going. "You okay?"

"Yeah. Be careful where you step."

She saw large chunks of colorful glass splintered into pieces on the floor. And Zach stood in the middle of the space with sweat running down his face, drinking from a water bottle. "What happened?"

"Too big." He wiped his brow with his forearm, and she saw that he was bleeding.

"You cut your arm."

He shrugged. "It's fine."

She hustled forward. "No, it's not. There's glass in there. I can see it from here."

He bent his arm and looked at it. "Huh."

"Do you have a first aid kit?"

"On the shelf." He pointed toward the bathroom.

She slipped off her fleece jacket and threw it on a chair. "It's roasting in here."

"Yeah." He walked to the window and opened it wider.

She exited the bathroom with a first aid kit. Sidestepping the broken glass, Ginger made her way toward Zach.

He held out his hand.

But she waved him away. "Just sit down and I'll do it."

He didn't argue. He sat on a stool and gave her his arm. Blood trickled down to his elbow and dripped onto the floor.

"Nice." She took a deep breath and set the first aid kit down. Her hands trembled a little, so she scanned the table. At the other end, she spotted small piles of colored glass sprinkles. They glittered in the overhead light. Pretty.

She dug out a pair of tweezers and then looked at him. "This might hurt."

He raised one mocking eyebrow.

Ginger gritted her teeth, scanned the mass of mangled skin scarring his left biceps and then blew out her breath. "Right."

The piece of glass sparkled in the light. Grabbing the underside of his elbow, her gaze flew to his when he twitched. "What?"

"Your fingers are cold."

She took another deep breath, and with the tweezers, she grabbed the glass splinter, yanked it out and then set both on the table. The piece of glass was the length of a bobby pin. His wound bled more profusely with that sharp shard dislodged. "Ewwww."

His face grim, he handed her the half-empty water bottle. "Pour this over it to make sure you got all the splinters out."

She did as he asked and then ripped open a large gauze bandage that she placed over the cut. "Hold that a minute. Can you tell if there's anything still in there?"

He looked at her. "It's good."

"Good." Ginger hopped up on the metal table and wiped her own sweating brow. "Blech."

He chuckled. "You look a little green."

"Not a big fan of blood."

Zach stood and grabbed a roll of paper towels. Still holding the bandage that was soaking through, he handed her the towels. "Dry off my arm, and then we'll put another bandage on there and tape it down."

She nodded. Tearing off a couple of towels, she patted his forearm dry, trying not to look up into his face, steering clear of his eyes.

"I'm sorry about earlier." His voice was whisper soft.

And it cut right through her. She shrugged, but cold air blew in from the open window and made her shiver. "It's okay."

"It's not."

She looked up and another shiver raced up her spine. Would he kiss her again? Part of her hoped…

He didn't. He handed her a fresh bandage. "Open that."

She nodded and her fingers fumbled with the packaging. Foolish girl!

He stilled her hands, until she looked up. "Friends? I won't pull that on you again."

Ginger battled both disappointment and relief. "Okay, friends."

"Good." He pulled the bloodstained bandage off.

The cut was already clotting. He'd live. Ginger laid the new bandage in place and while Zach held the gauze, she firmly taped the edges.

He gave her a crooked half grin. "Nice job."

"Girl Scouts, but I dropped out before I earned my medical badge. So, what happened?"

He ran his hand through his hair, making it stand straight up. "I was tapping a good-sized globe onto that knock off table and lost it."

She noticed a dark burn mark on the underside of his other forearm and touched it, but he didn't flinch. "Does it hurt?"

He shrugged again. "It's fine."

She searched in the first aid kit and found some antibiotic ointment. Twisting off the cap, she squeezed a dollop onto her finger. "Here."

"You do it." He held his arm out.

Was he teasing her?

She spread the ointment quickly across his burned skin, and her pulse picked up speed. Friends—right. Her heart wasn't supposed to skip beats with a friend. She didn't dare look at him or he might see how much he affected her.

She tore off a couple of sheets of paper towel, wiped off her fingers and then the tweezers. She scooped up the glass splinter with the towels and threw it all away. Glancing at the mess of broken glass on the floor, she asked, "Can you save any of that?"

He grabbed a broom and swept the pieces into a pile. "Nope."

She handed him the dustpan.

He scooped up the pile and tossed it in the trash.

"Now what?"

"I'll make another one."

Ginger chewed the inside of her mouth. She should leave, but didn't want to. "Can I help?"

He looked at her for a long moment and then finally said, "You want to give it a try?"

Ginger's stomach flipped. "Really?"

"I'll show you. Have a seat over here." He patted his workbench with the high sides.

She watched him slip that long metal pipe into the bigger furnace. The molten glass dripped like thick honey. He twirled the pipe and then rolled it along the edge of the big steel table that still had the first aid kit lid lain open at the other end.

Then he dipped the pipe in the furnace again, gathering more hot glass onto the already glowing glob. "What do you want to make?"

She grinned. "Another globe?"

He nodded. "What color?"

"All colors."

He gave her a nod and dipped the glob of hot glass into piles of colored glass sprinkles. He picked up a few blue, some green and yellow and then red shimmering bits, then back into the furnace. Explaining what he was doing as he went, he cautioned her not to touch anything until he said to do so.

When he had a nice little ball of hot glass with streaks in it, he wiped off the mouthpiece of a hose that was connected to the pipe. "Here, blow through this."

Ginger did as he asked.

"Harder than that."

She giggled and blew harder. The hot glass at the end of the pipe bubbled and leaned.

"Okay, roll the pipe along this ledge here. See how it lets the glass stretch."

She twirled the pipe too slowly, so Zach placed his hands between hers and rolled faster. She let loose a nervous-sounding giggle again. "This is so cool."

He took the pipe and twirled it in the glory hole furnace with its wide circular opening. He pulled it back out and handed her the mouthpiece. "Blow again."

She did as he asked while looking up into his eyes.

"That's good. See how it's filling out?" He rolled the pipe with her. "You want to keep going?"

"Yes. I want to do everything from start to finish. Show me everything."

He smiled at her. A full-blown wide smile that made her heart race. "Okay."

Time had stopped. Ten minutes or two hours, Ginger didn't know how long she stayed with Zach, blowing globes and then finishing up with a couple of vases. Her vase twisted really weird, but he said that he liked it and wouldn't toss it. He showed her how to use the giant tweezers he called "jacks" to pull the glass like taffy and then eventually cut it away from the pipe.

He was right there, protecting her, teaching her, even showing her how to shape the molten glass with wet wooden cups called blocks. Then he'd take over and together they'd take the piece to the knock off table, dislodging their glass creations from the pipe.

She felt like Alice must have after falling down the rabbit hole into a whole new world of color and shapes and heat. She understood why Zach called it hot work, but her fear of getting burned lessened as the night wore on. Zach was a good teacher, keeping her safe. But her heart had inched dangerously close to a different kind of fire. One that might consume her if she wasn't careful.

Finally, Zach donned heavy mitts and carried the last thing they'd made to the cooling oven. "We'll be able to handle everything in the morning."

Ginger yawned. "What time is it?"

"One thirty."

They'd been working for hours, but it had gone by so fast. "How'd you get into this?"

He went to the minifridge and grabbed two bottles of water. Handing her one, he said, "I attended a glass workshop while taking night classes and pretty much got hooked."

Ginger took a long sip. "Night classes?"

"I had to get my degree in order to become an officer."

"So what's your degree in?"

He gave her that half smile. "Business."

Of course, he'd trained for this, too. "So, how'd you fit it all in?"

He shrugged. "After transferring to another base, I finished my degree online. The glass-blowing met the humanities requirement, but like I said, I was hooked. I found an owner of a small glass studio who needed help and apprenticed with him when I was off duty in order to use his studio after hours. I did that for years. It's why I settled on a business degree. I wanted my own shop after I retired."

"So that's why you came home?"

A shadow passed over his face. He emptied his water bottle and tossed it into the recycle bin. "It wasn't my choice to leave the army this soon."

"What happened?" Ginger saw his stormy expression and backpedaled real quick. "I mean, if you care to share."

A flicker of something dark and angry shone from his eyes. "I received my walking papers while in Afghanistan. Latest round of budget cuts. Despite my exemplary service, I got RIFed."

Ginger cringed at the raw sarcasm in his voice, but wanted clarification. "Riffed?"

"Reduction in force. Let go, laid off, whatever fits."

"Oh. I'm sorry."

"Don't be. And keep it quiet. I haven't told my family."

"Why not?"

His anger turned to discomfort. "If I'd been a commissioned officer from the start, maybe I'd still be there. Like I said before, my father graduated from West Point. I was supposed to follow in his footsteps, but my grades weren't good enough. I enlisted instead, having no intention of becoming an officer. But then I was recommended for OCS—"

"What's that?" Ginger interrupted.

"Officer Candidate School. As a commissioned officer, a four-year degree is required. And since I was making a lifelong career out of it, I jumped at the chance to move up."

Ginger understood all too well. Zach wanted to live up to his father's example and make him proud. Didn't he realize he'd surpassed it by his active duty? She'd heard Helen mention that Zach had been deployed too many times to count.

"Didn't matter in the end. I didn't make twenty years. There's no way I would have retired without at least twenty years in. My dad knows that."

"He hasn't asked?"

"No."

"Maybe he's waiting on you to tell him."

Zach grunted. "Might be a long wait."

"Why? Don't you think your dad would understand better than most?"

He shrugged.

There had to be more to it than not fulfilling his career expectations. Getting laid off because of budget cuts wasn't exactly something Zach could control. But then, neither were his nightmares. Did his family know about those? Did the army?

In her opinion, getting let go from the army might be the best thing for him in the long run. It had to be. She'd read the joy in his eyes while he worked. His whole countenance lit up when he taught her the craft of working with glass.

And she'd responded back with joy. Ginger couldn't remember when she'd had so much fun. "Maybe that was God's plan to get you out."

He gave her a look that said she didn't know what she was talking about.

The grump had returned. And that made her defenses rise along with her voice. "I don't know what you were like in the army, but you're so alive when you're working with glass. I can see it's your passion. It makes you a good teacher."

He suddenly chuckled. "I'm not so passionate with the customers."

She laughed, too, relieved that he'd lightened the moment instead of biting her head off. "No. Not so much."

"Maybe that's where you come in."

She tipped her head. "Me?"

"Work for me."

Ginger's belly fluttered. Those butterflies were dancing up a storm. Zach was talking crazy and she was crazy enough to want to believe him. "I think the late night has gotten to you."

"I'm serious." He wasn't kidding.

And that scared her more than she'd like to admit. Time to leave. "No."

"Why not?"

She spread her arms wide. "I have my own business to run."

He took a step toward her. "*You* came alive shaping that glass. Tell me you didn't love it."

Ginger stepped back. He'd read her like an open book. Could he sense how he'd affected her, too? Coaxing out all kinds of wish-filled feelings that working for him might destroy?

She grabbed her fleece jacket and headed toward the door. “It’s late and I’m going to bed.”

“Yeah, it is late.” He turned off the light, closed and locked the door behind them.

She bounded up the stairs, unlocked the door to her apartment and then waited. “Thank you for tonight. It was fun.”

When Zach reached the top, he looked way too intent. “Think about it, Ginger.”

“Good night, Zach.” Ginger opened her door and slipped inside.

No way.

There was no way she could accept that offer and keep her heart safe. After working hard to make something of herself, she couldn’t throw it all away on the whim of a handsome man asking. A man she cared for too much but didn’t dare trust with her future.

The next morning, Zach stepped out of his apartment with coffee mug in hand. He’d slept well despite making glass into the wee hours. Maybe all that work had given him a dreamless night. Whatever it was, he looked forward to Ginger’s reaction to the items they’d made last night.

He paused at her door. Should he knock?

No.

He’d see her downstairs in the safety of their

respective shops. If he hoped to keep things on a friendly and professional level, he'd stay away from her in her apartment.

By the time he flipped on the lights at the back of his studio, he knew Ginger was already at work. He smelled the scent of cinnamon from the tea she'd made every morning this week before overhearing her talking on the phone to someone about the window contest, answering questions, giving advice. Must be another merchant. And Ginger was always ready to help.

He heard the click of her heeled footsteps as she entered his place through the slider. He never locked it, knowing she kept her side locked.

He met her near his sales counter. "Morning."

"Have you opened the cooling oven yet?" Ginger's eyes shone with eagerness.

"Not yet. Come on back." Maybe offering her a job hadn't been such a bad idea. She was clearly hooked. Much like he'd been all those years ago. Could he afford to bring her on? Sooner seemed better than later, but that might be the thrill of working with her last night. He needed to crunch the numbers and readjust his plan. She had a business to run and part of that was paying him rent. To hire Ginger, he'd have to take over her retail space and increase sales sooner than planned. Based on his traffic, he might be ready. But was he ready for Ginger?

Maybe…

He opened the doors of the annealing oven and reached inside. The glass was cool enough to touch, and gently, he withdrew the vase Ginger had made. It leaned a bit on one side, but he'd fortified the bottom so it would stand without toppling. She'd used the small jack to pinch the sides into a swirling twist of red and white and clear glass that he liked.

Her eyes widened. "Can I touch it?"

"You can have it."

She caressed the glass before taking the vase from him. Then she scrunched her nose. "It's not good enough to sell, is it?"

He chuckled. "Maybe not, but it's an excellent first try. More like what most come up with on their fourth or fifth lesson."

"Really?" She didn't look as if she believed him.

"I don't blow smoke, Ginger."

Her eyes narrowed, and he saw the satisfaction register deep in her brown eyes. "So, it's pretty good?"

"Very good." He pulled out the globes. One by one, they were bigger than what he usually made alone and loaded with twisted glass strands inside. Setting them in a wooden box he kept by one of the worktables, he added, "These will definitely sell, and I couldn't have made them without your help."

"Really?"

He gave her a look.

"Sorry. Not used to compliments. Especially coming from you." She gave him a playful grin.

He snorted. For a look like that, he'd do almost anything. "Just stating facts, but I'll compliment more often."

Her cheeks colored and she looked away. Setting aside her vase, she inspected the glass globes, touching each one. "You better put a decent price tag on them. Don't just give them away like you do with your little glass hearts."

He needed this woman in his shop. "I will."

"And you should hang them in your window."

He cocked an eyebrow. She needed to pick a display idea and make it into a reality. "For now."

Touching the large cobalt blue ball of glass with strings of glass embedded inside, Ginger smiled at him. "Right. For now."

Every thought about keeping it professional and friendly scattered. Remembering the feel of his lips on hers, he wanted to pull her close and make good on kissing her properly. And definitely more thoroughly than what they'd shared walking home last night.

As if reading his thoughts, she backed away, grabbed her vase and headed for her side through the slider. "I've got to run out for a second."

He glanced at his watch. Nine forty-five. They both opened in fifteen minutes. "What about your customers?"

She shrugged. "If I'm a little late opening up, no big deal. You're the one with the *groupies*. Entertain the ladies until I get back. Oh, and Zach. If Sally shows up, don't let her leave till I get back. I'll only be a few minutes."

"Got it." But he shook his head.

This was how it could be if they worked together. With Ginger's help, his business would grow. She was good not only with the customers, but pricing details and community stuff. He needed this woman to flourish. And he needed to convince Ginger it's what she needed, too.

Chapter Eight

By the time Ginger returned with baked goods and a bouquet of flowers, Zach's groupies were only a couple of women who looked disappointed as they left. "What's with them?"

Zach sipped from his coffee mug. "I'm not doing hot work this morning, so they left."

"Oh." Ginger raised the bakery box. "I've got Danish and doughnuts if you'd like some."

He grinned. "Yeah."

Ginger nodded for him to follow her. She set down the box on the table in her break room and put out little plates and napkins.

Zach dug in. "Thanks."

"Thank you for the class on glass last night. You're a good teacher."

"Yeah?" He looked surprised by that. The corner of his mouth lifted. "You're a good student."

Ginger's heart pumped hard. "Thank you."

"You're welcome."

Ginger checked her watch then bustled about filling her electric urn with water and then plugged it in. Did she imagine that Zach watched her every move? She turned around to check, but he was grabbing another goodie from the box. "Sally should be here soon."

He nodded. They both heard the jingle of bells, and Zach made a move to leave.

"I'll see who it is. Eat your Danish." Ginger hurried out and spotted Sally standing in the middle of Zach's retail space. "So, what do you think?"

Her previous landlord, mentor and friend smiled. "This is lovely, just lovely. He's done a lot of work. Where is he?"

"In the back." Ginger thumbed toward her shop but then she felt Zach's presence behind her.

"Morning, Sally." He stood right next to her and offered his hand to the elderly woman, brushing lightly against Ginger's arm in the process.

Did he have to stand so close?

And Sally smiled as she shook Zach's hand. "You two get along well, I see."

"Uh, yeah." Zach spoke first. "Would you like the full tour?"

"I'd love one, yes." Sally grabbed Ginger's

hand and squeezed. "I'm so glad to see you are well, dear."

Ginger squeezed back. *Well* might be a relative term subject to interpretation considering the roller coaster of emotions she'd been on in the past twenty-four hours. "Thanks, Sally."

"And he's a looker, too," her dear friend whispered, only it was loud enough for Zach to hear.

He cocked one eyebrow at her, waiting for a response.

"Yes." What else was Ginger supposed to say?

Zach was indeed handsome, but after last night's kiss that left her wanting more, and then his teaching her how to work with glass, she was in a bit of a tailspin. His invitation to work for him was tempting. But not all temptations were healthy.

"Now, tell me how all this works." Sally pointed to the furnaces and workbench.

"Ginger can tell you while I wrap something for you." Zach went to his counter and grabbed a wad of Bubble Wrap.

Sally glanced at her with wide eyes. "You know all this?"

Ginger felt her face heat, and she glared at Zach's back. "Some. He showed me a few things about making glass..."

She didn't admit that it was last night. Instead she launched into a quick explanation of the process. Gathering the hot glass from the main furnace, rolling it on that tabletop called a marver to pick up colored chips, back in to gather more glass, then blow or shape.

Sally's smile grew wider. "I see. You seem to like this glasswork."

Ginger's cheeks blazed even hotter. Sally saw too much, and the more Ginger tried to hide her feelings, the more they rose to the surface. "I guess I do."

"Sally, come pick out a vase to take." Zach opened the annealing oven where the vases they'd made stood proud and pretty.

Ginger was never so glad for Zach's interruption.

"Oh, my." Sally inched closer and pointed. "I'll take that blue one. Blue's my favorite color, you know."

"Nice. I'm partial to red, these days." Zach gave her a wink.

And Ginger wanted to disappear. Captain Zach certainly knew how to flirt when he wanted to. And she didn't want him flirting with her in front of Sally. The woman already had ideas in her head about them and might spread that around town. But then, hadn't he made a show of it at the chamber meeting?

Something she'd wanted for real?

She clenched and unclenched her fists while Zach gently wrapped the vase and slipped it into a bag and handed it over to Sally. The bells on his entrance door jingled again as a couple of customers ambled inside, stamping their boots and brushing off snow that fell in fat flakes.

Sally patted Zach's hand. "Thank you. I'll let you get back to work. Ginger, shall we have tea?"

Ginger nodded, glad to escape but afraid of what Sally might think. "Of course. And I have your favorite doughnuts, too."

"Oh, good."

"Don't forget to show Sally the vase you made," Zach said.

"Will do." Ginger couldn't get back to her side fast enough. "What kind of tea would you like? I have this spicy new chai blend."

"No, no, plain black tea, please. But show me this vase first."

Ginger grabbed the vase she'd made with Zach. She had purchased a bundle of red, pink and white carnations from the florist after picking up doughnuts at the bakery. "Right here."

"Oh, Ginger, that's beautiful."

"A little lopsided, but Zach said it was a decent effort."

"Honey, he cares for you."

Ginger coughed. "What?"

Sally touched the twisted vase of red, pink and clear glass. "Why else would he show you how to do this?"

Because he wants me to work for him. Ginger shrugged. "Because I asked him to."

Sally nodded with a knowing smile. "Well, it's good to know you're in good hands here."

He raised the rent. But Ginger wouldn't tell Sally that, either. She'd only worry. "Yup. Good hands."

"Now show me this new tea. Is it selling?"

"So far, but I bought it for Valentine's Day. I hope to sell gift baskets."

"And what about your window? Do you have any ideas for the contest?"

"I'm working on it." But Ginger was stumped.

"Maybe Zach will help."

"Yes." She handed Sally a cup of plain tea and the honeypot. Ginger didn't tell her about their window deal. Sally might blab to her friend June, and Ginger really didn't want the whole town to know that.

Sally patted Ginger's hand. "You always make up such nice displays. You'll do fine."

"Thanks."

But Ginger wasn't so sure. A romantic theme

was much tougher than a Christmas display. At least, for her. She'd always feared falling for someone. Afraid she'd give up control in her life. Afraid she'd find nothing but heartache and rejection.

Digging deep for a window display contest dredged up all those fears because Ginger was afraid to showcase her girlish dreams. Because some dreams never came true.

By the end of the day, Ginger wanted to give up on window ideas and settle for the usual hearts and arrows. Walking to the front of her shop, she stared at the expanse of glass. People bundled in their winter best walked by outside as snowflakes swirled in the fading light of day.

She glanced at the vase she'd made with Zach, now filled with that cheerful bouquet of carnations. She'd stared at that flower-filled vase all day. If she went to work for Zach, would she really learn the whole art of glassblowing? Or would he keep her tied to the cash register and waiting on customers?

Thinking of those flowers, so perfect for Valentine's Day, Ginger wanted that simple perfection for her window. And Zach's. But how? What decorations would suit them both?

"What do you see out there?" Zach's deep voice rumbled from behind her.

He'd been busy today, and that meant she'd been busy, too, helping with his customers. His offer to work for him nagged like a sore tooth, throbbing with interest. She couldn't muster the courage to ask if he was serious. Asking meant she'd considered it.

Working for Zach might be an easy way out of her financial struggles, but it was also the quitter's way out. She'd trade one set of headaches for another. What if Zach's nightmares took over until he couldn't function? Was that possible? He'd planted the thoughts about going "postal," and that worry had taken root even if it never bloomed.

Nope, Ginger knew what to expect with her own set of problems.

She let out a frustrated sigh. "That's the trouble, I can't see anything good. Not good enough to win, anyway."

He stood next to her, arms folded, and stared out on to Main Street, as well. "Bring out what's in your heart."

Ginger laughed, but it sounded bitter even to her ears. "Nothing romantic in there."

"Come on." He looked at her.

She recalled their brief kiss. Looking back,

it wasn't much of a romantic kiss. Not really. He'd kissed her to shut her up, and she'd only started to kiss him back when he ended it.

Yup, Captain Zach was a regular Prince Charming.

And *that* was wish-filled thinking.

Just like this newfound desire to make glass. With him.

Ginger placed her hands on her hips and faced him. "Okay, smarty-pants, what's in your heart?"

Zach gave her that half smile. "Icicles and Novocain."

She searched his face. Sure, he joked, but the sad thing was maybe he was right. She imagined that he'd had to numb his feelings pretty good to do what he'd had to while deployed. Once frozen, did emotions ever really thaw?

"Then it's no wonder you're no help."

He shrugged. "Don't worry. You know what this town will want to see."

"Yeah, maybe."

"Hey, I gotta run out to my parents' place. See you tomorrow."

"Sure thing." Ginger gave him a wave, but her attention remained fixed on the window. She had only a week to figure it out.

* * *

Sunday morning, Zach entered the sanctuary of Ginger's church with his brother Matthew, Annie and her baby. He and Matthew found seats in the back, and Zach stood closest to the side aisle where he wouldn't be boxed in. He could view the entire room, including all the exits. The church was medium-sized and old, with long wooden pews and tall clear windows topped with stained glass. Nice. Definitely not too formal.

He spotted Ginger on the platform wearing a soft-looking dress that was neither brown nor gray but a mix of both. It kissed her curves as well as the top of those high-heeled boots.

She saw him and smiled.

His pulse picked up speed.

She stood between a woman and a man, and they sang while a small band played a simple chorus. He knew the words and joined in but stopped when the baby started to fuss.

Annie made her way by him and then headed for the nursery.

He gave his brother a curious look.

Matthew leaned and whispered, "He's hungry again."

Zach chuckled. The kid was a tank. One that ran through fuel like water.

Matthew and Annie had been late picking him up, and that was a good thing. With the song service already started, he didn't have to mill around in the foyer and meet a bunch of people. Ginger would have been the one introducing him, too, and that would have looked too much as if they were together.

Which shouldn't matter because he'd found himself considering that more times than not. The past couple of days she'd helped him way more than he'd expected. Not only waiting on his customers, but after hours she'd helped with the hot work. She'd held some large custom pieces while he made adjustments.

Eager to learn the basics, Friday night she'd assisted him in making dozens of small glass hearts and replicas of her vase in preparation for Valentine's Day.

He'd incorporated the odd twist she'd accidentally created into the center of some larger heart ornaments. Ginger had been surprised by that, as if she still didn't believe that he liked the effect. He'd already told her he didn't bother with words that were not true. What he hadn't said was that she wasted her talent in a dying tea shop.

Another song ended. It had been a contemplative tune and Ginger opened her eyes and stared right at him. Through him. He didn't look away. Keeping a friendly distance was getting tougher. They saw each other every day during business hours, and now that bled into after-hours work, as well. Friends would never cut it.

He didn't want to be her friend.

But romance came with a high price. He'd have to let himself feel, and that made him vulnerable—to disappointment, to anger and loss. He didn't want to pursue her only to lose her in the end because he could share only so much of himself, could feel only so much. There were times when he wanted silence, times when he sat staring at nothing. Was it fair to pursue a woman so full of life, when deep down, he believed he shouldn't be alive?

Zach made it through the next couple of worship songs that were simple choruses he knew well. He had sung many over the years at various church services. But when the next song started, he didn't recognize the tune. It started out fine, referencing all the reasons to bless the Lord's name.

But then the haunting melody took over and the band stopped playing, leaving only the piano until that guy stopped playing, too. The voices of everyone in that sanctuary blended together and the volume rose. The purity of sound and genuine emotion hit him hard. A combination of worship and need, nothing was held back. Nothing numbed or ignored.

And God was right there in the midst of such terrible honesty.

Zach felt the hot stab of conviction. His conscience tore at his heart, slicing that organ to shreds. Ginger's voice, along with those of the other two singers, was lost in the gathering of sound and spirit lit with cleansing fire. He didn't want to listen. Didn't want to feel the tugging on his heart to open up.

He jiggled his leg and clutched the edge of the pew in front of him. *Jesus.*

Zach begged for calm but found none. Iron sharpened iron and God wasn't knocking lightly. Like after waking from a nightmare, Zach's breathing came hard, so he sat down. If he could shut down, maybe block it all out, he'd be fine, but it took everything he had to keep his butt in the pew.

He leaned forward. Resting his elbows on his knees, Zach closed his eyes and prayed. Hard.

But it hurt. This wrestling within his soul.

Gripping his hands together, he felt something like tearing within him and nearly cried out. The door to his heart had grown rusted shut, and it felt as if God used a crowbar to get in there. Gritting his teeth until his jaw ached, Zach started to shake. All over and uncontrollably.

He felt his brother's hand on his shoulder. Matthew squeezed hard. "It's okay, man."

But it wasn't.

Might never be.

Zach was going to lose it.

He stood, grateful the other parishioners had remained standing and were too lost in the song to notice him. But just before he hit the aisle, he connected with a pair of wide brown eyes.

Ginger looked scared.

He was scared, too. Horrified that he might crumble into a bawling mess. That was a place no soldier wanted to go. Especially in public.

He got out of there as quickly and quietly as he could. Once outside, he booked it across the parking lot, into the field beyond, and fell to his knees. He slammed his bare fists into a frozen chunk of piled snow. Two more times, he punched the icy snowbank until the cold burned his knuckles and the crunchy crust scraped his skin.

Spent, he hung his head and cried.

After watching Zach hightail it out of church, tears poured down Ginger's face. She thought she'd heard something from outside, a sound so raw and painful it had made her cry. Was that Zach? Or the swirling crows cawing in the trees beyond the window? Those sorrowful bird calls tugged at her heart, too. As if something or someone had died.

The song ended and she glanced at Matthew, but his head was down. No doubt, praying for his brother.

Would Zach come back?

What should she do if he did? Even worse, what if he didn't? Should she sit in her usual spot or go outside and try to help? What had happened and what could she really do about it?

Her pastor grabbed the microphone and gave announcements, signaling the end of the worship service.

Stepping off the platform, Ginger spotted Annie slipping into the pew next to Matthew while she cradled her sleeping infant. He whispered something in her ear, and Annie looked deeply concerned.

Oh, no. Maybe Zach had flipped out.

Ginger sat down in her normal front side pew and grabbed her purse. She mopped her face with a couple of tissues and prayed, but her sorrow turned into fear when Zach still hadn't returned by the time the offering had been taken. Was Zach dealing with a flashback or something?

Would he hurt himself?

She suddenly felt sick.

And then reason took over. Okay, Zach might

be short-tempered, but she didn't believe he was a violent man. But by greeting time, Ginger could stand it no longer. She popped up and quickly headed for the back of the church. She'd run outside if she had to.

Suddenly, Zach entered through the push doors from the foyer. He looked calm enough, but his hair was damp, as if maybe he'd washed his face in a hurry.

Ginger stopped and stared.

He looked back for what seemed like minutes when it couldn't be more than a few seconds. His eyes looked a little red, but he gave her one of his half smiles.

Her knees threatened to give out in relief. Her eyes burned with another round of tears threatening to fall, and she went to him.

"Don't," he warned.

She sniffed and nodded. This might be the place, but it wasn't the time. Not for Zach.

The pastor was at the podium again, asking them all to return to their seats for a quick hymn before the message.

Zach headed for his place at the back pew.

And Ginger stood frozen, watching him slap Matthew's back as if nothing out of the ordinary had taken place. As though he hadn't left church as if the building was on fire. Helpless, she stood still, her feet refusing to move.

He looked up and caught her gaze. His blue eyes were fierce and focused. Whatever had happened, Zach was back in control. He scooted over in the pew, causing Matthew and Annie to do the same. He patted the spot next to him. He'd made room for her and expected her to obey his simple command to sit.

Still, she hesitated. What if she couldn't help it and asked what happened after he'd warned her not to? What if she cried? Worse, what if he freaked out again?

He cocked one eyebrow at her. Challenging her.

And that shook her into action. Most everyone was seated now, and she wasn't about to tromp back to her pew way up in the front. So Ginger walked to the back.

Zach didn't slide over. He'd slipped back to the edge of the pew closest to the aisle.

Seriously? Did he expect her to shimmy past him?

He expected exactly that and the glare he gave her said so.

She quickly pushed her way through, her knees knocking into his, and settled into the spot between him and his brother.

Her pastor instructed everyone to open their hymnals and sing "It Is Well with My Soul."

Zach reached for the book and Ginger saw

the scratches on the backs of his hands. Her heart twisted as she ran her fingers across his swollen knuckles. “Oh—”

He grabbed her hand and squeezed hard.

Zach wanted to shut her up again. He didn’t want her calling attention to his reddened skin. He didn’t want her sympathy. Or her tears. Maybe he didn’t want her…

She pulled her hand back and leaned against the pew. Her pulse erratic.

He offered to share the pages of the hymnal, but Ginger could barely sing for the lump lodged in her throat. She listened to him, though. Zach’s voice sounded deep and smooth, and in control.

It is well, with my soul.

It is well, with my soul.

It is well, it is well, with my soul...

As they sang, Ginger turned the words into a prayer. For Zach. Whatever he’d been through over there, fighting for his country and hers, Zach’s soul had been torn up far worse than his hands. Worse than the angry, puckered scar marking his arm.

She leaned close, sharing the pages of the worn old hymnbook, even though she knew the lyrics by heart. She found her voice and gave it everything she had.

He glanced at her, eyes wide.

And she raised her eyebrow in challenge.

There'd be no shutting her up from this song. She sang for herself, too, a pledge that she was okay. Proof that by trusting in God's love a person could rise above the pain. Then she made it back to a prayer for him. She hoped that one day, Zach might repeat this hymn with real conviction.

But that might be more wishful thinking, because the question in her heart remained, scratching with worry—would Zach ever be whole?

Chapter Nine

Zach climbed into the passenger seat of Ginger's red Beetle and waited for the inevitable questions that were bound to follow. Ginger wore her emotions clearly on her face, and she'd looked worried sick. For him. And he couldn't decide whether to be warmed by that or irritated. He'd find more protection in the latter, but couldn't quite rouse the effort it took to be mad.

Matthew and Annie had dinner plans with the baby's grandparents and Zach couldn't see them backtracking to drive him home. Not when Ginger was already headed there, so he'd asked her for a ride. And she'd agreed.

He braced for whatever she might have to say.

So far, she hadn't said a word. She started her car but didn't pull out. She cranked the heat and let the car idle. Rubbing her mittened hands together, she remained silent.

He couldn't stand it. "Go ahead."

She looked at him. "Go ahead and what?"

"Ask me. Or should I just admit that I couldn't handle the worship service today?"

She bit her bottom lip. "Why? Why couldn't you handle it? What happened, Zach?"

He shrugged. "Honestly, I don't know."

"Was it a flashback?"

He shook his head. "No."

"Did you have another nightmare last night?"

He leaned his head back and sighed. "No."

Again silence settled like a blanket of newly fallen snow between them. But he knew better. He knew *her* better, and she was rallying her troops, ready for a full-out charge.

The sound of the defroster running on high grated on his nerves, so he reached over and turned the knob down to Low.

Ginger gave him a do-not-touch glare and turned it back up, only not as high as before, and she switched it to floor heat. "Why do you dream like you do?"

He let out a bark of laughter. If he knew that, maybe he wouldn't have them so often. He wasn't about to give her all the gory details but figured he owed her something. "I led my men into an ambush. I could have taken a different route—I almost made that call before our convoy rolled out. I didn't."

Ginger's gaze narrowed. "You couldn't have known."

"I knew the area. I knew enough."

"Zach—"

He held up his hand. "Spare me. I've heard it all. None of it changes the fact that four good men died because of my indecision."

"Are your nightmares about that ambush or different?"

"I relive it every time. Same conclusion. Same deaths. Same dream."

"Did the army find any fault with your orders?"

He ran a hand through his hair. He'd received commendations and that only made it worse. "No. They didn't. Still gave me my walking papers, though."

"So you think blaming yourself is the answer."

"Maybe." He should have been the one to take that hit. Not his sergeant.

"But it was war. How could it be your fault?"

He knew that, too, on some level. But that mental knowledge didn't begin to touch the way he felt. He was single. Alone. Those men had families, wives. He'd seen pictures of their children. Some with the family pet. "Tell that to my sergeant's wife and his three kids."

"Is that who you were thinking about this morning?" She slipped off her mittens and adjusted the heat to Low.

Zach looked out the window. He'd been thinking about Ginger. "No."

"Have you talked to your father about this?"

"God or my dad?" Zach chuckled.

Ginger gave him a sweet smile that warmed him more than the heater. "Well, both I guess."

Zach nodded. Why'd he fear talking to his own father? "I might have worn God's ears off this morning."

"But not your dad's."

"No."

"Surely he'd understand better than most."

"Yeah."

Ginger touched his arm. "Then why not talk to him?"

Because he couldn't handle seeing recrimination in his dad's eyes once he knew the situation. Zach could have changed the route. He'd ignored a hunch. He'd gone with the plan and men had died. He couldn't change that basic truth. He was to blame no matter how he sliced it.

"Our minds can be a battlefield all their own." Her voice held quiet conviction. As if maybe she spoke from experience.

That didn't sit well with him, either. They

hadn't moved from the church parking lot. The interior of her car was warm now, but also suffocating in its closeness.

Nowhere to hide.

But he didn't want to leave. Not yet. Not until he discovered what lay behind Ginger's sunny-blue-skies gumption. "So, you choose to be positive. Look at the bright side of things?"

"I have to be."

"Why?"

Ginger looked at him. "Would you like to grab something to eat somewhere?"

His gut turned. "Long story?"

"Not really, but I'm hungry. And I know a great place for breakfast if you're interested."

He nodded. "I am."

Ginger pulled out of the church parking lot, but instead of heading for Maple Springs, as he thought, she drove the opposite direction.

And Zach got that tense feeling in the pit of his stomach. Not nearly as bad a sensation as he'd get during mission briefings, but along the same lines. What secrets did Ginger harbor behind that cheerful facade of hers?

Did he really want to know?

Ginger slid into the vinyl booth of a small diner she'd discovered when she'd attended college. It smelled like strong coffee and sizzling bacon. The chef made funky pancakes of the day ranging from Key Lime to carrot cake. Since they were in the mood for breakfast, the choice had been an easy one.

The conversation wouldn't be. She was about to let Zach know what made her tick, and it didn't feel so good. If knowledge was power, she was about to give her landlord a whole lot of knowing why she was who she was and what she feared.

A waitress appeared with a pot of coffee and poured it into Zach's mug.

"Tea for me, please." Ginger looked over the pancake specials listed on the wall and smiled. "And I'll have the chocolate pancakes with raspberry sauce, as well."

Zach shook his head and ordered the big breakfast complete with a side of plain cakes.

"You'll be happy to know they serve real maple syrup, but it's not your dad's."

"Monica's pushing our parents to supply the local restaurants, but my father does things his way and for now that's craft fairs and the Maple Springs IGA."

Ginger nodded. "So that's where you get it from."

"Get what?"

"Stubbornness."

Zach laughed. “Take a look in the mirror, sweetheart.”

“I’m not stubborn.” She ripped the wrapper off her straw then dunked it in her glass of ice water. “I’m persistent.”

“So, that’s what you’re calling it? Whatever you are, you were going to tell me why you’re so positive.”

She twirled the straw wrapper between her fingers until it made a tiny white paper ball. “If I don’t look at the positives in my life, if I don’t constantly count my blessings and stay grounded in what’s true, I’ll believe every lie my father told me.”

There. She’d said it. And it sounded so trivial compared with what he’d been through, but she wanted to help him, somehow. If that meant baring her soul a little, then she’d do it.

Zach took the straw paper away from her and stilled her hands with his own. His touch was surprisingly gentle, as was his voice when he asked, “What did your father say?”

Ginger looked into his blue eyes and saw concern there. “He said I’d never amount to anything and was bound to be a quitter just like him.”

Zach’s gaze turned cold and steely. “Why would he say that, and more importantly, why would you believe it?”

"I quit every sports team I ever tried out for, I nearly flunked out of high school and I dropped out of the junior college I attended right here, in this town. Oh, and I quit the Girl Scouts, but I already told you that."

"You were young."

Ginger wasn't interested in excuses. "I'm not so young now. The only thing I have to show for myself is that tea shop. I own a business in Maple Springs, Michigan, and that means something."

Zach let go of her hands. "Is that why winning the window thing means so much?"

"I could really use the statewide advertising. I need my shop to survive."

"You're a smart woman, Ginger. You don't need that shop to prove you're something special."

Easy to say, but did he really mean it? Words had the power to hurt or heal. So, maybe she'd given too much power to the words spoken to her all her life. But Zach's sweet words couldn't erase years of rotten ones.

She sighed. "It means something to my family. To my father, anyway. It's the one thing he can't diss. Maple Springs is a place of success. Closing up shop would only prove his point that I failed and quit one more thing in my life."

Zach glared. "You've nothing more to prove."

But she did. "I'm the reason my father had to drop out of school to provide for my mom and me by driving a truck. Not to mention my brother almost died and can't hear out of one ear, also because of me." Ginger cocked her head. "Don't you see that I need to win at something?"

Zach looked as if he'd sucked a sour lemon. He didn't say anything, but Ginger could easily imagine his thoughts. He probably thought she was too sensitive or overly emotional. He'd proved his worth in action. He was a returning war vet. A man of valor and honor despite the guilt he carried around like a sack of cement.

"You have a wonderful family, Zach. And your father loves you. No mistake you think you've made could ever change that."

"Now we're back to me." His eyes grew stormy.

"Yeah, I guess we are." If only she could make him see the pride Andy Zelinsky had in his son. It oozed out of the man like the maple syrup he made. "Have you considered that the reason you haven't talked to your dad is that he'll tell you straight up you're not at fault? Then you'll have to forgive yourself for—"

His eyes narrowed. "Coming home alive."

Ginger's stomach tripped and fell. She

couldn't fathom why he'd ever believe that he should be dead, but knew it was a lie. And lies could sometimes feel like truth. She swallowed hard. "I had two choices growing up. I could believe my dad or prove him wrong."

Their food arrived and intruded.

"Want me to pray?" she offered.

He shook his head. "No. I'll do it."

Was he afraid of what she might pray for? Ginger closed her eyes as Zach recited his family's dinnertime prayer.

When he'd finished, Ginger touched his hand. "I haven't faced anything close to what you have, but believing those men died because of you is not truth."

"How do you know?"

"Whoever ambushed you—Taliban?—they killed your men. Even if you had changed the route, who's to say the same thing wouldn't have happened along another road?"

He stared at her. Obviously these were things he'd already considered, but couldn't rest in. "Why'd I come home with barely a scratch?"

Ginger didn't think that scar on his left arm could be counted a mere scratch. "Because God has plans for you yet."

His eyes widened and he gripped her hand. It wasn't a touch to shut her up. It was the grateful kind of touch that said *thanks*.

* * *

Later that day, Zach stared at their windows. What theme would Ginger choose, and would it be good enough for her to win? After she'd dropped him off, Ginger had changed her clothes and then hopped back in her car for a two-hour drive to Traverse City. She wanted decorating supplies and hadn't asked him to go with her.

Not that he would have gone along, but a change of scenery might have been good. They could have grabbed dinner somewhere, but then, that probably wasn't a good idea, either.

For simplicity, he kept the same store hours as Ginger and most of the surrounding gift shops. He was open Tuesday through Saturday and closed Sundays and Mondays. Summer months, Ginger said she opened The Spice of Life on Mondays, too, but Zach wasn't into that. He liked having two days in a row to himself.

Ginger worked hard. And she'd stay anchored to her sinking tea ship to prove that she could. He might accept her idea of success if she loved what she did. But he didn't believe she did. He'd seen that spark of excitement in her eyes when she worked with glass. The passion that came with making new things and the same things with new twists.

Ginger deserved to win, but Zach wasn't sure

about her ideas. The suggestions she'd made so far were nothing to get excited over. But then what did he know? He'd never owned a gift shop before. And he was no whiz when it came to marketing. His sister Monica said as much, when he told her to back off from such a fancy website.

God has plans for you yet...

Ginger's words had paraphrased a scripture he'd clung to for years. Did she confirm what God had promised? If so, was this studio part of a bigger plan that might include her? Or was there more?

A knock at the door interrupted his thoughts.

Zach spotted the sporting goods store owner from next door, outside, holding a box. He opened up. "Can I help you?"

"This came for Ginger yesterday but was delivered to my place. The sales kid placed it on my desk and I just found it."

"Thanks. I'll make sure she gets it." Zach looked at the label from a ceramics company.

He carried the box into his store and laid it on the counter. Ginger still kept the slider locked on her side when she wasn't around. As building owner, he had keys, but if Ginger didn't trust him enough to leave her side unlocked, then she'd have to pick up her delivery here.

Another knock.

His father stood outside, looking in.

Zach opened the door. "What's up?"

His dad nodded. "I needed a few things at the hardware store and thought I'd stop by. Are you busy?"

Not yet he wasn't. He had glass to make, but that could keep for now. "Come in."

His father was a tall man, trim yet still fit. He had a serious demeanor and wasn't comfortable standing around. "I thought we could walk."

Zach's eyes narrowed. This sounded serious. "Let me grab my coat."

By the time they stepped outside into the winter sunshine, Zach was worried. "Is Mom okay?"

His father wrapped his arm around Zach's shoulders and squeezed. "She's fine, but she's concerned about you."

Maybe the time for talking to his father had finally come. His mom had pushed for it, and so had Ginger only this morning. Coincidence? Probably not. "I'm fine."

Right.

"What happened, son? Why are you home so early in your career?" His father waited patiently.

Zach took a deep breath and blew it back out, making a smoky cloud of frozen breath in front of his face. He and his father walked toward the waterfront where the small harbor lay shrouded in snow-topped ice. No boats were moored at the docks. Many were stored in the boat shop parking lot and wrapped in bright blue plastic, lined up and waiting for the spring thaw.

"I've been RIFed. Got the letter while I was over there on my last deployment."

His father nodded. "I'd heard there'd been deep cuts."

Zach thought he'd try to practice a little of Ginger's look-at-the-bright-side attitude. "Didn't get my twenty years but I had over eight as a captain, so I'll stay a captain when it comes to retirement pay, even though it's less than it would have been in another year. Some of the other guys who'd commissioned late weren't so fortunate."

"You served your country well, Zach. Don't let being forced out make you think otherwise."

"Sure, Dad." But how could he not think so?

His father stopped walking and faced him. "I mean it, son. I know you lost good men a few years back. As a leader it's not easy to accept loss of any kind. But you have to focus on your gains, or you'll get eaten alive by the could-haves."

His father spoke from experience. His special ops unit had been part of the team that had invaded Grenada. His father had also lost men under his command. Zach had been little then, but he remembered snippets of stories heard on the news and clipped conversations over the phone.

He also remembered his mom's frantic pacing. She'd tried to protect him from the details, but never once did she gloss over the reality that his father was in harm's way. Even then, she'd clung to her faith and encouraged Zach to pray as well.

Zach nodded. Those could-haves were killers. How many times had he relived what he did and what he could have done until it had made him crazy? Ginger had said the same thing as his dad, but how was he supposed to find that shift when he couldn't redo what was done? It wouldn't make a difference to those families.

This morning at church, he'd finally given in to the pain. Maybe God had waited for him to break before Him so his heart could be softened. All that anger and guilt had frozen it up solid, but would the nightmares stop now that he'd melted? Now that he'd opened up some?

He looked his father in the eyes, not seeing his dad but the lieutenant-colonel he'd been. The military figure Zach had always admired and the reason he'd enlisted. "Do you ever dream about it?"

His father's eyes widened in pain, but he

didn't look away. "Sometimes. Even after all these years. What are these dreams you have?"

Zach sighed. Maybe he'd live with the nightmares forever. But maybe getting his father's view of where he'd gone wrong might help him accept what happened. Now more than ever, Zach needed his father's insight, even if he'd hear where he'd made mistakes.

"The nightmares are the ambush. It's like a skip in a movie that plays over and over."

They started walking again, past the boat shop with its storage area and lifts, toward the summer homes of Bay Willows that were closed up for the season. They walked the shoreline sidewalk and their footsteps crunched through snow. The cold air made Zach's nose run.

His father nodded. "Have you talked to a VA counselor?"

Zach shrugged. "Yeah, but—"

His dad touched his shoulder. "But not since coming home."

"No."

"I have a good friend at the VA here. He's been where we've been."

Zach leaned his head back. "I'm talked out."

"You haven't told me. Tell me what went down."

Looking into his father's stern blue eyes, Zach saw his superior instead of his dad. He'd get a fair hearing. One he could believe. One he was afraid to hear.

Good or bad, Zach had to know his father's reaction. He was ready for it. "I ignored a hunch and followed orders, taking the planned route. I could have changed it. I could have postponed and regrouped."

"Why didn't you?"

Zach braced for the disappointment, the recrimination he knew should come. "I didn't trust my instincts. The scout team had given their clearance. I was tired, pushed to get this mission done, so we could get out of that hole. I went with it."

His father's eyes held understanding. Nothing more. "Sounds like that hunch might have been a natural case of the jitters. Zach, you were acting on the best information you had at the time."

"But it was a different feeling than other missions and other movements."

"How far were you before you got hit?"

Zach shrugged. "Not far. Not far at all."

"Maybe your intel was right and this group planned to attack the base, and your convoy got in the way."

Zach blew out his breath. "Maybe."

"That could have been worse."

All conjecture. Zach wanted to be blamed for something. He'd come home in one piece.

They turned away from the shoreline, walking up a short street that cut away from Bay Willows back to year-round residential homes. When his father stopped before a small ranch surrounded by a white picket fence, Zach knew they were headed here from the start.

And his hackles rose. "What's this?"

"There's someone I'd like you to meet." His father's eyes held nothing but hope.

Zach considered balking, but something in his father's expression made him stay and give in. He followed his father through the gate up to the front door.

It opened right away, before they even knocked.

"Andy." A guy limped toward them.

"Rob, this is my son Zach."

Zach knew Rob was a returning vet. Not hard to guess, taking in the prosthetic leg and haunted stare. He held out his hand. "Good to meet you."

Rob took it for a firm shake. "Yeah. You, too. Come on in. I just made coffee."

Zach looked at his dad. There'd be no backing out now. "Sounds good."

"Andy says you opened up a glass studio."

"Yeah. You should stop by sometime."

"I will."

Entering Rob's home, Zach experienced a sense of relief, and maybe even a feeling of rightness. He needed to be here right now, meeting this guy. Maybe Zach was finally ready to talk.

And his father looked proud.

Ginger dragged bags of newly purchased decorations into her break room. Zach had challenged her to dig into her heart. So she had. But because that gun-shy organ seemed filled with wishes, she went with her girlish dreams of what romance should be. Moonlight and stars and fireworks.

She heard a tight *rap-tap-tap* on the glass divider and knew it was Zach. Her pulse skipped a few beats. She shoved her bags on the shelf and walked around to the slider and opened it. "Hey."

Zach looked drained.

She wanted to push back his hair but clenched her hands into fists instead. "You okay?"

He gave her a half smile. "I talked with my father today. My earthly father."

Ginger smiled over the hitch in her throat. Why'd seeing this strong, impatient man so subdued make her want to cry? "Did it help?"

"He gave me perspective. And introduced me to a guy that goes to the local VA."

"Are you going to go, too?"

Zach nodded. "Yeah. I think I might."

Ginger wanted to jump and down, but she stayed cool instead, taking his admission to seek help in stride. Whatever had happened this morning at church had been a good thing. A very good thing.

"Did you find what you were looking for in TC?"

She took his quick change of subject for what it was. Zach wasn't up for digging deep, so she gave him a cheerful smile. "I did. Here are the receipts for you, too."

"So, what did you decide?" Without even looking at them, he stashed the folded thin paper receipts into his pocket.

Her stomach flipped at the softness in his voice. "Not telling. You'll see it when I have it all up and in place."

His eyes darkened. "That good, huh?"

Ginger thought so, but she wasn't giving anything away. "It's the usual Valentine's Day stuff. You know, stuff the town wants to see."

He looked at her closely a moment more before gesturing toward his store. "There's a box over here for you."

"My teapots!" Ginger flew by him.

Running her hands over the huge box, she looked around the counter for scissors. And then looked at him.

Zach handed her a Swiss army pocketknife that looked way too sharp. "Here."

She scrunched her nose. "Will you do it?"

He chuckled and sliced through the tape.

Ginger pulled out plastic packing pillows and then finally boxes with ceramic teapots shaped out of two hearts with a wrought iron handle. She'd ordered them in Valentine's Day colors and set a red one on Zach's counter. "Aren't these awesome?"

He picked it up. "Kind of small."

"They hold two cups. Get it? Two hearts, two cups, one tea."

He looked at her, like really looked at her. "Two hearts blended into one."

And Ginger's breath caught. "Romantic, huh?"

"Yeah. I think so."

Ginger got the feeling they weren't talking about her teapots. The space around them seemed to shrink and the air grew tight. She glanced at his mouth, wishing for a better kiss than the one they'd already shared. If she leaned close, what might happen?

"Go with me to Matthew and Annie's wedding this Saturday."

"Sure, I'm already going." Ginger looked forward to seeing her friend given away by her late husband's parents. Annie and Matthew had decided not to have attendants, and Ginger was happy to just be a guest.

"Be my date." Zach's voice was whisper soft.

"Your date?" Her voice squeaked.

"Yeah."

Ginger's cheeks flushed, and she retreated to the safety of teasing. "You better watch it or your icicles might melt."

His face looked grim, but there was mischief in his eyes, too. "Maybe they already have."

She tipped her head. "That's good then, right?"

"Depends on your answer."

Ginger hoped he couldn't hear her rapid heartbeat pounding like a base drum inside her chest. The smart part of her wanted to refuse, but that wishful side looking for dreams jumped at the chance. "I'd love to be your date."

"That's good." Zach echoed her words, but then his eyes shone with concern. He was thinking too much. Or maybe she was.

Did he regret asking her?

Sure, it was only a family wedding, but they were going together. As a couple. Like two hearts blending into one. They were taking that big step forward.

Her stomach dipped and fluttered. Ginger hoped she didn't regret saying yes.

Chapter Ten

Zach woke drenched in sweat. This was getting old. Really old. With a groan, he got up. He didn't feel as shaky as he normally did after dreaming. But then, tonight the dream had been different. He'd been the one torn in half, and Ginger had pulled him out of her red Volkswagen.

Padding into his small kitchen, he then filled a glass with water and chugged it. Ginger had charged into his dreams, trying her best to save him even there. He peered out the window onto dark streets below. A lone runner with red hair streaming out from under a knitted hat jogged toward the high school.

Ginger.

The urge to throw on his clothes and join her tugged hard, but he ignored it. He needed to take things slow. He shouldn't race after her every chance he got. He searched Main Street and his gaze snagged on the icicles hanging from the roof of the building across the street. They looked like glass.

Recalling Ginger's reaction when he'd asked her out, he chuckled. Those dripping icicles reminded him that he was definitely thawing. Ginger had melted away his resolve to be just friends. He wanted more and wasn't sure if that was good or bad.

Either way, it made sense for them to attend his brother's wedding together. It was supposed to be a small gathering at the nearby Maple Springs Inn. The wedding provided an easy opportunity to ask her out and a neutral place where they could have fun without the pressure of being alone. It'd make a good first date.

Glancing at the clock, he decided he might as well stay up. At six in the morning, he'd had a full night's sleep in spite of dreaming. His day off and he couldn't sleep in. Maybe he'd never sleep late again. Wide awake, he changed into shorts and a T-shirt and lifted weights. Then he ran on his treadmill before popping into the shower.

By the time he made it downstairs to his shop, he spotted the beginning attempts by Ginger at decorating her window for Valentine's Day. The small café table with two chairs had been placed near the far wall and corner of the window. Covered with a frilly lace tablecloth, the table had been set with two red teacups and one of her new double-heart-shaped teapots, also in red. A basket of loose tea wrapped in heart-covered cellophane sat next to the teapot. The teddy bears were gone. Nice. He looked forward to what she'd come up with for the windows.

His cell phone buzzed to life and his heart froze when he spotted Darren's number. It was early for his brother to call. "Hey."

"Your shop is closed today, right?"

"Yeah."

"Good. Grab your sled gear and meet me at Mom and Dad's. We're hitting the trails pronto."

"Who is?"

"Just us guys. Hanging out before Matthew gets married. Even Luke drove up last night. Mom's having a fit that he's skipping classes today and tomorrow."

Zach laughed. He could use a day away from everything. Especially away from a certain red-head who turned him inside out. "Why didn't you call last night?"

"I did. I left you a message, didn't you get it?"

Last night he'd worked in his studio. He

wouldn't have heard his phone ring and hadn't checked it for messages before coming upstairs. "Yeah, probably but— It doesn't matter, I'll be there."

"Great. Thanks, Zach."

"See you soon."

Zach gathered what he needed into a small duffel. His snowmobile gear remained at his parents' house along with the sleds. The last time all his brothers had been together was right before the last deployment of his career. They'd gone camping a few days before Darren's wedding—the wedding that had never happened because the bride took off with the best man the night before the ceremony.

Zach had pitched in to help make those awkward phone calls to friends and family informing them the wedding was off. It wasn't fun. But then weddings were not exactly a barrel of laughs to begin with—at least not for him. This one might be, with Ginger as his date.

He flipped off the light and exited.

Ginger came in from outside and practically ran into him as he locked the back door to his studio before leaving. Her cheeks and nose were red and her brown eyes wide with surprise. "Morning."

"How was your run?" He felt himself smiling. One of these days he'd join her.

"Good."

"I'm taking off to snowmobile with my brothers. Do you need anything before I go?"

She gave him a fierce look. "Why would I need anything?"

He laughed. "Look who's grumpy. Just being polite."

"Guess I'm not used to that—you being polite." Her eyes teased.

"Nice." Zach's gaze strayed to her lips. "Maybe you're rubbing off on me with all your positivity."

Ginger grinned at him then. "Yeah?"

"Yeah." He needed to get moving or he might kiss her right then and there. And that would make him late for sure. He gestured toward the top landing and their respective apartments. "Ladies first."

Ginger nodded and tore up the stairs. At the top, she spun around, her face flushed and beautiful. "Hey, be careful, okay?"

Zach's heart skipped a beat or two as he looked up at her. Warmth spread through him, melting those icicles some more, making him smile. "I will."

Ginger smiled back and entered her apartment with a soft close of the door.

She cared.

He did, too. But he wasn't sure what to do

about it. Like any objective with variables, he needed to think it through and be sure. The last thing he wanted was Ginger getting hurt.

The following morning, Ginger headed downstairs to open up her shop. With her rent check clutched in her hand, she hoped Zach didn't mind that it was two days late. She also hoped he was home.

As usual, Zach had left his side of the slider unlocked, giving her open access to his shop. Yesterday, she'd had a field day with the windows. Uninterrupted and able to focus, Ginger had created starlight and moonshine with strings of tiny white lights swathed in rhinestone-studded tulle. But she'd hated that every sound she'd heard had made her heart jump in anticipation of seeing Zach.

She'd wanted his thoughts on the windows, but as far as she knew he hadn't returned from his snowmobiling trip. And that meant he'd missed seeing the decorated windows at their best. At night.

She opened the slider and stepped inside his retail space. Nine thirty and no lights shone from his side. "Zach?"

"Yeah?" He stepped out from the back of his workspace with a steaming mug of coffee in hand. His hair looked damp from a shower and his eyes tired.

"You just got in?"

He nodded. "About fifteen minutes ago."

"You don't look like you slept." Ginger hated the worried sound in her voice.

He didn't look a bit sorry for it. "Not much, no. We ended up at my cousin's house and stayed. He lives right off the snowmobile trail."

Ginger's eyes narrowed. So it wasn't nightmares that stole away his sleep. He certainly didn't owe her an explanation for staying out all night, but a simple phone call would have been nice and might have put her mind at ease.

"What'd you need?"

She could tell Zach wasn't in the mood to chat, but he could at least mention the windows. Tamping down irritation, Ginger handed over the check. "February's rent. Sorry I didn't make the first."

His eyes grew serious in an instant and his cheeks colored a little as he took it. He stared at the check, and then at her. "You've got till the tenth of the month, so no big deal."

"Before a late fee kicks in." Ginger didn't know why she wanted to rub that in.

"Right." He tipped his head. "You okay?"

It wasn't Zach's fault that check had nearly wiped out her checkbook balance. Just as it wasn't his fault that she'd waited up for him hoping he'd see the decorations and worried that he'd get hurt out there on the trails. Snowmobiles were fast these days.

Ginger let out her breath. "I'm fine."

"I noticed what you did with the windows." He sipped his steaming black coffee. "It looks nice."

She clenched her fists behind her back. Just nice? What wasn't he saying? "It's better at night, you know, with the lights."

"Yeah—" A knock on his front door interrupted.

Checking her watch, she realized it was time to open. She backed away and headed for the woman bundled in a fur-trimmed parka waiting to come in. It was one of his glassblowing groupies—the older woman who'd written the article. "We'll talk later."

He nodded.

"No glass making today?" the woman asked.

"Not this morning. What can I help you with?" Zach took care of the woman's hunt for a pretty vase and even chatted about the weather and when the article would run in the local gazette.

He sounded like any regular store owner. One who didn't need her help.

Ginger headed for her tea shop to make up

gift baskets. Away from fishing for Zach's approval on the windows. Away from the disappointment that gripped her. Their deal was over.

Well after lunchtime, Zach walked through the slider to Ginger's side. He'd had good traffic for a Tuesday morning and a few good sales, but it had quieted down to nothing the past couple of hours. Ginger hadn't peeked in since they'd both opened their doors.

He spotted her behind the counter, typing away on her laptop. "Playing games?"

She gave him a wry smile. "Going through month-end figures might be considered a game of sorts."

"Maybe this will help." He handed her a check.

"What's this for?"

"Reimbursement."

"But this is more than I spent."

"You never told me what your time was worth, so I guessed. That's for waiting on my customers."

Her pretty brow furrowed. "Zach, I can't accept this..."

"Just take it, Ginger." Accepting her rent check earlier had been weird. About as weird as she looked right now scanning the check he'd given her.

Getting involved with her when there was a rent payment between them made things feel sticky. Stickier still were the windows. It looked like a bridal store with all that net stuff. He understood the silvery-looking moon, but what were those big silver spiky things supposed to be? Several different sizes, she had them hanging all over but more so above that little tea table of hers.

He had to change it if they wanted to win, but how could he do that without playing right into her hang-ups? Wars were won despite losing a battle or two, and Zach couldn't let this one go. He had to make sure she won that contest. But would winning be worth bruising her pride in the process?

"I'm going to grab a sandwich. Do you want one?"

Ginger shook her head. "No, thanks."

"Come on. Eat lunch with me and then let's do some hot work. It's not busy. We can make more hearts."

She looked at him with desire in her eyes. Like a kid wishing to play outside instead of being stuck doing homework inside. "I've got stuff to do."

He knew he had her. "Do it later."

She sighed and nodded.

"Chicken club?"

She shook her head. "I have leftovers."

"Eat those later." He winked at her and left.

It didn't take long, and when he returned with their bagged lunch, he heard Ginger tinkering in the back room. He stepped behind the counter in order to join her, but her opened laptop caught his attention. The document she'd been working on was still on the screen—a spreadsheet with too many red numbers in parentheses.

He stepped closer and frowned.

Ginger's trends didn't look good. In fact, her shop wasn't only in trouble. It was failing.

Ginger heard the crinkle of paper and looked up as Zach entered the back room. She'd set the table with paper plates and napkins along with a salt and pepper shaker. She'd placed a ten-dollar bill on the table, too.

Looking grim, Zach set the bag down and picked up the bill. "I don't want this."

"You paid last time."

He pushed the money toward her. "So?"

"So, why can't I pay?" Ginger pushed it back toward his plate.

"I'm not playing this game. Keep your ten," he growled.

Ginger glared at him. He'd paid for breakfast the other day and then gave her a check that was too much, and now he wouldn't let her pay for her own sandwich. "Are you trying to bribe me or something?"

He laughed. "What are you talking about?"

"I can pay for my own lunch, Zach."

He grabbed the ten and shoved it in his pocket. "Better?"

She nodded. "Better."

"And you're not stubborn." Zach slipped into the chair across from her.

"Persistent." She bit into her sandwich.

Zach ate fast and quietly. No chatter when there was glasswork to do.

Still, his lack of enthusiasm for her window display shriveled up her appetite. She wrapped up the uneaten half of her sandwich for another time and slipped it into her little fridge.

"You might want to change your clothes."

She fiddled with the hem of the wool sweater she wore. Working with glass, the temperatures got pretty hot. "Watch my shop?"

He nodded. "I don't think anyone's coming in, though. It's snowing pretty hard out there."

"I'll be right back." Ginger exited the back room and charged up the stairs to her apartment.

Once she was dressed in a T-shirt and jeans,

she locked her front entrance and hung a note to inquire next door for tea. She didn't want anyone wandering around where she couldn't see them from Zach's workspace.

She glanced outside. Heavy snow fell and the streets were in fact empty. Very few shoppers were out and about, but that was okay. The voting for downtown windows didn't open until the upcoming weekend.

A week before Valentine's Day.

She entered Zach's space and slipped onto the workbench. She watched him roll the molten end of the pipe into bits of colored glass frit on the marver before heading back to the furnace to reheat. He twirled the pipe a few times before dipping the end in for more honey-like hot glass.

His movements were sure and relaxed. He'd taken off his sweater and wore only a T-shirt with faded blue jeans. That wicked-looking knight tattoo of his peeked out from underneath Zach's short sleeve as he leaned forward. And just like that conquering image in ink, Zach had marched right into her heart.

"Here, hold on to this." He placed the pipe across the side rails of the workbench. "Roll it."

She did as asked and he grabbed a bunch of folded wet newspaper and shaped the blob. Steam rose around his hands and a few sparks flew. He took the pipe, gathered up more glass and returned. She twirled while he shaped the form.

They repeated this dance a couple more times until he grabbed the jack and pulled the hot glass into the shape of a heart. The glass shone opaque but still yellow hot with flecks of pink showing through where the edges grew clearer. Then he added that twist in the middle. The one she'd accidentally achieved with her vase.

She looked into his eyes, getting lost there.

He looked back. "I told you I liked it."

Her heart pulled like the hot glass he manipulated. "I want a go at the next one."

He gave her that half smile and placed his hand over hers. "Twirl."

She rolled the pipe with his hand still on hers, and he used the jack to indent the glass enough so he could eventually break off the heart with a few taps.

Okay, maybe she'd gotten the windows all wrong. Love wasn't moonlight and stars and fireworks in the sky. It was something much closer, and uncomfortable. It smoldered hot like the consuming fire of the furnaces behind them. Her feelings for Zach were scary. Her heart was no different from the pretty glass hearts they'd made. Fragile and easily broken, could she trust Zach not to shatter it?

He took the pipe to the knock off table and tapped the hot heart onto a special pad. Using a hand torch, he reheated the one side of the glass and smoothed it out with a file.

"Next one is yours." He donned a pair of mitts and placed the heart in the cooling oven.

Ginger stood, grabbed the pipe and dipped the end in as he'd shown her. And they repeated the process. Zach stayed close, gently coaching and showing her small variations to the work.

"Nice job," he said after they'd made a couple of dozen or so of the hearts.

"What's next?" Ginger couldn't get enough.

Zach chuckled. "We close up shop and keep going for a bit. If you want to."

Ginger hesitated. Distance might be a good thing right now before she fell in line and followed Zach anywhere. "I better not. I need to get some paperwork done."

"Right." His eyes were on her with concern, but he didn't say anything.

Ginger stood and glanced outside. The sky had darkened to a deeper gray. Snow continued to fall and the streetlamps had come on. It'd be dark soon. Her tiny white lights flickered to life from the auto timer and bathed the front of the studio in soft, warm light.

She scrunched her nose. “Well, what do you think?”

“I think you should let the tea shop go and work with me.”

“You’re serious.” Part of her wanted to, but that voice of caution kicked in and kept her from jumping at the chance.

“I am.”

She shook her head. “I don’t know, Zach. That’s a big step.”

“I know.” He gently gripped her shoulder and squeezed. “Think about it.”

“Okay. Now, honestly, what do you think of my window display?” Watching him, she knew she’d gone and blown it. Why’d she have to dig for more than nice? Why couldn’t she settle for nice?

She held her breath while he really looked at the front of his shop. He’d stepped out into his retail space so he could scope out her window, too.

She followed him. “It looks better from outside.”

“Yeah, probably true.”

She swallowed the bitter taste of hurt. “So you don’t like the windows.”

"The windows are fine, but you're wasting your time and talent in a dying tea shop."

She stared at him, trying to read between the lines of what he said, but he spoke plainly enough. There was no malice in his voice, no mean-spiritedness either. He simply stated his opinion as if it shouldn't tear her in two.

"You asked for honesty."

"That I did." Ginger nodded, but his answer stabbed deep. And no way would she let him see how deep. "How do you know it's dying?"

He raised one eyebrow. "Your back shelves are bare."

She forced a laugh and even smiled. "But it's wintertime. My slow time of year."

His eyes saw right through that excuse. His studio had been busy since the day he opened. "You want to stay and keep going? I could use your help."

She shook her head. "I really need to get back to my month-end work. Thanks, Zach. I'll see you tomorrow."

She barely heard his reply as she hurried next door for the last half hour before she closed up for the night. Gathering her laptop so she could finish upstairs in her apartment, she heard Zach turn up his radio. He'd continue blowing glass.

Part of her wanted to join him. She wanted to believe that he wanted her to work for him because she was good, talented even. But what if that was wish-filled thinking on her part? She'd built her own business, but it wasn't successful. She barely made ends meet, so what was the point anymore?

The other part of her that had run from an even smaller town and away from her dysfunctional family wanted to prove Zach wrong. She didn't need him or anyone else telling her what she could and couldn't do.

Zach was only one person with one opinion. The proof she needed was wrapped up in the window display contest. If she won, she'd finally have the chance to showcase her store on a statewide level. And then she'd know for sure.

Chapter Eleven

By Saturday, Zach knew what he had to do, but finding the right time to do it was another matter. He'd spent the rest of the week making items needed to transform their windows in time for voting. Finding an opportunity when Ginger wasn't around proved nearly impossible, so tonight, after his brother's wedding, he'd work through the night if he had to.

She might not be pleased, but in the end, when they'd won, she'd have the ability to advertise and maybe grow. At the end of the year, when Ginger's lease was up, he hoped she'd know if the win was worth it. At the end of the year, he wanted her to close up her shop and apprentice with him. But he wanted her to want that, too.

At six o'clock, after he'd locked the front door

to his studio, he stepped through the slider into Ginger's. "Will you be ready in half an hour?"

"I will."

"Good. I'll see you soon." Zach headed for his apartment.

He wanted a shower and a shave. His mom had said the wedding wasn't formal, but he'd wear a suit anyway. This was his and Ginger's first date. He wanted to look nice.

Twenty-five minutes later, he knocked on Ginger's door.

She opened it and smiled. "Hey."

He took in the gorgeous red dress she wore with long sleeves and a full skirt that skimmed her knees. She looked like a valentine. His valentine. He lingered on her feet encased in deadly high heels of man-slaying leopard print and shook his head. "We better drive."

"I can walk."

He laughed. "In those things?"

"They're really comfortable and the sidewalks are clear."

They'd had an early February thaw the past couple of days and tonight the temperature had stayed mild and well above freezing. "Let's go."

"I'll get my coat." She left the door open.

He watched her slip into a long wool coat, and her hair blazed against the black fabric.

She pulled on fuzzy red gloves that made him smile. She was a living flame, this girl.

"What?" She looked up and cocked her head.

He shrugged. "Nothing."

"You were looking at me weird."

He leaned close and whispered, "Because you look amazing."

"Thanks. So do you." She blushed and brushed past him to pull the door shut behind them. "Come on, let's go."

He smiled at that admission. She seemed a little distant lately. Jumpy even, if he got too close. So he'd back off, like now. Not teasing her. He followed her down the stairs, and once they were outside, he made a grand show of offering her his arm.

"Whoa, who are you?" She made an equally grand show of slipping her arm through his.

"A man on a date."

Laughing, she actually snuggled a little closer.

And Zach was a goner.

He wanted Ginger to become part of his business, but the more he pushed, the more she retreated. So, he'd let the matter drop. He'd invited her to help him make more twisted glass hearts with the excuse that he'd sell them long after Valentine's Day.

He didn't let her know that she helped him

make the items he'd use to redo their windows. The more they'd worked side by side this week, the more Zach wanted to make that kind of arrangement permanent.

Ginger couldn't stop glancing at Zach after they'd arrived at the inn and he'd hung up his overcoat. He wore a gray flannel suit like nobody's business. With a smoothly shaved jaw and piercing blue eyes, the man looked as if he'd walked off the pages of a magazine.

He led her into a small private room where the wedding ceremony would be held. Despite the warmth of his hand against her back, she shivered.

"Cold?" He slipped his arm around her waist.

"I'll warm up." She hoped he hadn't noticed how she'd trembled when he drew her closer to his side. One peek at the man who'd caused it and his face remained serious as he scanned the room.

A young woman played a harp in the corner of the room. The soft sounds soothed as Ginger scanned the rows of white folding chairs without a separation down the middle. There were no ushers to lead them to their seats, so it was up to them to find a spot. "Do we have to choose sides?"

"Huh?"

"You know, the bride's side or groom's side?" She looked around. "If so, I need to sit on Annie's."

He shrugged. "You lead the way."

Ginger headed to the left and slipped into the middle seats of the middle rows. Looking around, she noticed that many of Zach's family were seated all over. Annie's sister had come all the way from Arizona with her husband and their two small children. They sat in the front, but that was it when it came to Annie's family.

Ginger figured that Helen Zelinsky had probably erased that middle line of demarcation in the seating. A seemingly small thing, but incredibly thoughtful. Annie didn't need any reminders that her family was scarce in numbers.

Zach fidgeted next to her. He turned and looked around, then leaned close and whispered in her ear. "Mind if we move to the end of the row?"

She shook her head. "Then people will have to climb over us."

He ran his hands against his thighs. "I don't like the middle. I can't see what's behind me."

"You're at a wedding."

"Old habits die hard." He got up and moved.

Ginger considered staying put, but then someone might think they'd been arguing, and she didn't need that. Not when most of the folks attending were Zach's relatives. She moved toward him. "You'll be sorry once this room fills up and someone steps on your toe."

He draped his arm around the back of her chair, pivoting in his, so he could see the way they'd come in. He scanned the room thoroughly before relaxing. "This is much better."

She narrowed her gaze. What threat could there possibly be in Maple Springs? But Zach was serious. He'd been conditioned to anticipate trouble and be prepared to deal with it.

He'd gone to the VA office this past week and had asked if she'd watch his retail space while he was gone. She'd been glad to do it. Anything to ensure he found the truth in his actions and made peace with it.

The night of the open chamber meeting, Zach had made the right call with Lewis. He'd known that guy wasn't dangerous and had stood down. Though not without making a show of staking his claim.

Ginger briefly closed her eyes, as her skin tingled with the memory of Zach so close. And that snippet of a kiss…

"Excuse me."

Ginger looked up at the man wanting to get by. Talk about getting caught in a daydream.

"This is my uncle John." Zach was standing,

too, giving her an odd look. "Ginger has a shop next to mine."

Ginger stood as well and shook the man's hand. "Nice to meet you."

"Pleasure." Zach's uncle gave her a knowing wink. "Keep this guy in line, you hear?"

She felt her cheeks heat, but played along. "Sure thing."

The room filled up fast. And with each person who needed to file by them, Zach not only stood to let them by, but thanked them for coming and introduced her as he did with his uncle.

When their row was finally full and he sat down for the last time, Ginger relaxed, mumbling, "The power of a suit."

"What?"

"You're quite the charmer with all that grateful-host stuff."

"That's why I sat here," he whispered near her ear. "To show you that I can be cordial."

She knew that wasn't true but accepted it as a good enough excuse. Zach might be out of the army, but would the army ever be out of him? Glancing at his strong profile and eyes that took in everything around him, she doubted it. Zach protected his own. And that wasn't a bad thing. Not at all.

He noticed her attention and winked.

And that caused the butterflies in her belly

to dance. If she worked for him, would he turn army captain on her, barking out orders and missions for each day? He'd been a patient teacher, but who knew what kind of employer he'd make. She liked making her own decisions, but she'd loved making glass, too.

Her church minister entered the room from the side, as did the wedding party. Annie had chosen her late husband's parents to stand up with her instead of a bridesmaid. And Zach's parents acted as best man for Matthew.

With Annie dressed in a beautiful yellow party dress, it wasn't the traditional sort of wedding, but she carried a small bouquet of dark pink roses and yellow tulips and looked every bit a glowing bride. And Ginger felt her throat close up tight.

The ceremony was short and sweet. When the minister pronounced Annie and Matthew as man and wife, Zach grabbed her hand. "Get ready to scoot out of here as soon as they walk by."

She dabbed her eyes with a tissue.

"Are you crying?" He sounded horrified.

She sniffed and laughed, making the tears run over and dribble down her cheeks. "I can't help it. I'm happy. For them."

"Come on." Zach grabbed her by the hand and they exited through a side door.

"Wait, what about the receiving line?" Ginger glanced back at the small mob of guests waiting to congratulate the newly married couple.

"We'll talk to them at dinner." He gently tugged her forward.

Holding fast to Zach's hand, Ginger followed. "So, where are we going?"

"You'll see."

He led them down the stairs to the lower level and through a long hallway toward the sound of jazz music. They exited a door and were outside, but the pathway leading to a large garden pavilion was completely protected by sturdy clear plastic and lit with tiny white lights. Outdoor heaters kept the area cozy while a swing band played and people danced.

"Are we crashing another wedding?"

Zach smiled. "No. This is one of your chamber's Valentine's Day specials set up for this weekend and next. I can't believe you didn't know about it. Brady announced it at the meeting the other night, remember?"

Ginger must have missed that announcement at the open meeting. But then, that was the night Zach had attended and he'd snagged her thoughts and attention all evening. The evening that had ended with a kiss to shut her up.

Zach hadn't missed that announcement,

though. And he'd not only remembered it, he'd brought them out here on purpose. To dance. Would he kiss her, too?

Should she let him?

Ginger scoped the area. Hors d'oeuvres and a huge bowl of punch had been set up on a small round table in a corner opposite the band. "This is really nice."

"I know. Dance with me."

"Okay."

He swung her into his arms. And Ginger's breath caught when the tempo changed to a slow, languid tune and he pulled her even closer.

"Relax." His lips grazed her ear.

Easy for him to say. She felt like a tea bag heading for a pot of boiling-hot water. "But the wedding."

"We'll join them soon." He pulled back and looked into her eyes. Then he brushed his thumb against the corner of her eye.

"Thank you." Her heart raced at the tender expression on his face.

"I didn't think you'd want a smear of eye makeup."

She tipped her head back and smiled. "No, I mean, thank you for remembering about the band, and your suit, and—"

"This is our first date. I want it to be memorable." He ran his fingers through her hair, his eyes dark and intent.

If that wasn't romantic, she didn't know what was, but she panicked, a little. "Zach, I don't..."

"Shh." He cupped the back of her neck and drew her close and covered her lips with his own.

Gentle at first, he kissed her thoroughly, properly, and melted every bone in her body. She'd waited for this moment all her life without even realizing it. It was like watching the grand finale of Maple Springs's famous Fourth of July fireworks, or finding that missing puzzle piece after a long search. Contentment filled her.

This felt like coming home the way a homecoming should feel. Safe and loving as if she belonged. Maybe she did belong to this man and he to her. Maybe with him, she had nothing to prove other than her feelings.

With a surge of courage, she offered those up right along with her heart. Ginger returned the most perfect kiss she'd ever received and hoped for the best. She hoped Zach got the message and maybe had one of his own to tell.

Zach pulled back and rested his forehead against hers. "Wow."

"Yeah. Wow." Ginger closed her eyes but couldn't rein in her tongue and went looking for answers. "Why'd you do that?"

Zach laughed low and soft. "Because, you inspire me."

Her courage shriveled up. No declaration of affection with promises of more? She'd have even taken a crass "you rock my world."

Her eyes flew open. "What?"

"Come on." Zach took her by the hand and led her back the way they'd come.

She'd offered him her heart and he was inspired? To do what? He hadn't kissed her again, so she certainly hadn't inspired a repeat performance. What on earth had he meant? And what should she do now?

When they entered the reception room, the wedding guests were already seated for dinner. She spotted Annie and Matthew making the rounds. Matthew held the baby, and the little guy grinned and giggled and played with Matthew's ear.

Zach let go of her hand so he could pull his brother into a hug, baby John and all. "Congratulations."

"Thanks."

As the two brothers pounded each other's backs, Ginger's thoughts swirled in a million directions.

Annie leaned close. "You look like you're on cloud nine."

"More like cloud confusion." Ginger gave her best friend a hug. "And you're gorgeous."

"Thanks. So, what's the trouble?"

Ginger waved it away. Now wasn't the time or the place. "Oh nothing, it's nothing. Really."

But Annie glanced at Zach and then back at her with raised eyebrows. "Looks like something."

"I'll call you later in the week." Ginger shrugged and moved on with Zach to their table. The newlyweds were putting off their honeymoon trip until after the baby was older, so Ginger would have no problem following up as planned. Maybe Annie could help her make sense of these mixed-up feelings.

Zach pulled out a chair for her.

Again, she gave him a quick look of surprise. "Thank you."

He leaned close and whispered, "You're welcome."

When he sat down, he pulled her chair closer to his. Who was this charming man whom Zach had become?

A man on a date.

Ginger tried to focus on eating her salad, but she kept glancing at Zach. He looked more relaxed than she'd ever seen him as he talked easily with his cousins and younger brothers seated around them. They laughed and joked and recalled details of their night of snowmobiling that had served as Matthew's bachelor party.

Zach draped his arm around the back of her chair and made lazy circles just above her elbow with his fingers. It felt as foreign as it did familiar. And it worried her all the more. They'd crossed over to a couple in an instant. Like those old movies with the trains, she felt like a speeding train that had switched tracks. Were they on the right course? The one that went for miles, or the short track that ended with a crash at a huge blockade?

She heard the low vibrating hum of her cell phone in her small clutch of a purse on the table. She fumbled to check the caller's number and saw that it was her mom. A nugget of concern lodged in her throat. Her mom rarely called.

She let it go to voice mail and leaned toward Zach. "I've got to check on this call."

"Everything okay?"

"I don't know yet."

Her stomach knotted when her mom called again and she hurried into the hallway before answering. "Hello?"

"Ginger! Ginger, you have to come home..."

"Mom, calm down. What's going on?"

"We're in the ER and they want your dad to

stay over and have surgery. I don't know what to do… There are insurance papers and doctors—you gotta come home."

Ginger paced the lobby floor until she got the whole story. Her parents were at the hospital because her father had chest pains. She could hear her father's voice in the background, yelling at a nurse that he was leaving.

And her mother sounded close to hysterical.

"Okay, Mom, it's okay, I'm coming. I'll be there soon." Ginger disconnected and hung her head.

Zach touched her shoulder. "What is it?"

She groaned. "I have to go. My dad's in the hospital and my mom's freaking out. Sounds like he had a heart attack, but I don't know yet."

"Let's go. I'll drive."

She touched his arm. "No. Stay here with your family."

"Ginger—"

"Really, Zach. I could hear my father cursing a blue streak. He's not at death's door. I'll be fine. I'll stay a couple days and make sure everyone's okay."

"I'll walk you home then."

"Please, don't." She needed to prep for what lay ahead, and she'd rather do that alone.

He took her phone and punched in his contact information. "Call me when you get there. I don't care how late."

Then he caressed her cheek.

She pressed into the palm of his hand. "I've got to go."

He looked concerned, but nodded, and then gave her a feather-light kiss. "Be careful."

"I will, thanks."

She hustled toward the coatroom and realized she needed to hit the ladies' room on her way out. Once inside the stall, she heard voices and froze when Zach's name was mentioned.

"So you think he likes running a business?" a young woman's voice asked.

"I think so, most of it anyway."

Ginger easily recognized the voice of Zach's sister Monica. She strained to hear over the sound of running water at the sink.

"But he needs more space to do what he really wants to do. The other night, I overhead him telling Dad that he wants to offer some classes. Sooner's better than later, but he has to convince Ginger to let go of that tea shop before he can expand."

Ginger's ears rang.

"What kind of classes?"

Monica laughed. "Glassblowing, what else? But he said he wants to keep it low profile for now. No mention of it on his website. He needs her help with customers and the community to really grow it, make sure folks are on board. You know how he is."

"True."

Ginger's heart pinched tight. She didn't move a muscle until well after Zach's sisters left, and then it felt as if her feet had turned into cement blocks. Washing her hands at the sink, she peered at herself in the mirror.

She was a foolish girl with foolish dreams that were sinking fast.

Could she really believe Zach's sudden charm was because of feelings he had for her? His offer to work for him seemed tainted now, as if she was a means to an end. Her end.

Oh, she inspired him all right, and that inspiration might put her out of business.

Chapter Twelve

Zach checked his phone as he walked home. Ginger should have gotten there by now. He couldn't remember the name of the Podunk town where she'd grown up. She'd said it was smack-dab in the middle of nothing and only a couple of hours south of Maple Springs. It'd been three and a half hours since she'd left the wedding reception, and he hadn't heard a peep.

He glanced at the clear black sky above dotted with a million stars and a shining-bright half moon. The temperatures had climbed into the high forties with almost balmy southerly winds. A perfect night for a romantic walk. But he was missing the girl. And it hit pretty hard that it felt as if part of him was missing with Ginger gone.

His phone buzzed to life. "Hey."

"I made it. I'm home." Ginger sounded weary.

"You okay?" He didn't like hearing the fire in her sound as if it was flickering out.

She sighed. "Yeah. I practically had to drag my mother from the hospital. She's afraid my dad will walk out the door."

Zach regretted not going with her. He had a few words for her father. "If you need me, say the word and I'm there. I can leave right now."

Silence.

"Ginger?"

"Thanks." She sounded distant, as if rallying her strength for battle. "But that won't be necessary."

"Even so."

"It's late. I've got to go."

"Keep me posted." Zach didn't want to hang up. He had so much to say to her but didn't know how to start. He'd never been good with words.

"I will." Ginger hesitated, as well. They stayed connected, neither one saying anything until finally she softly said, "Good night, Zach."

"'Night."

He pocketed his phone as their storefronts came into view. Tiny white lights and shiny netting and those silver things that looked like explosions dangled behind the glass. It wasn't a bad display, it simply didn't say much. He needed to make over both windows in time for open voting on Monday.

He had all the time in the world with Ginger gone home to her folks. But that contest win didn't seem nearly as important as showing Ginger what was in his heart. He'd once told her that place was full of icicles. But that wasn't true anymore.

She'd made him feel again. She'd given him insight to his future. Maybe even the reason he'd come home alive. He wanted things he'd never wanted before. And as daunting as it was to thaw, Zach had never run from a fight.

Securing Ginger's affection was one battle he planned to win. Starting with a message in their windows.

The last time Ginger had been home was Christmas Day. She'd driven down in the morning and returned by nightfall, in and out before anyone got hurt. Especially her. Although she usually left with a sore spirit, tonight she'd arrived with a bruised heart.

Hearing Monica talk about Zach wanting to convince her to give up her tea shop stabbed of betrayal. Was Zach's offer to work for him about her abilities or the fact that he wanted to take over her retail space? All that talk about what her time was worth—had that been his way of figuring out a wage she couldn't refuse? His comment about being a man on a date sounded awfully close to a man on a mission. Much too close.

She ran her fingertips over her bottom lip, remembering the sweet pressure of his kiss. The way he'd held her when they danced, as if she were dear to him. She'd felt cherished.

She glanced at her mother leaning against the kitchen sink with an unlit cigarette hanging from her mouth. "Keep that up and you're not far behind Dad."

Her mother shook out of the trance she'd been in and stared at Ginger as if she spoke a foreign language.

Ginger might as well be foreign and out of place in her childhood home. Her mother had never understood why she'd moved up north. "They're going to tell Dad to stop smoking. And you should, too, so he doesn't inhale it secondhand."

"Oh, he's not going to like that."

"No, he won't." Ginger clenched her teeth.

Her mom whipped out a cheap lighter and sucked until the end caught and smoldered. Did she really want to go through this all over again? What was her dad's life worth? "So are you going to quit?"

Her mom shrugged. "Not yet, and he ain't home right now."

Ginger ground her mouth shut before she said something she'd regret.

Her brother stumbled in, home from a party, and looked surprised. "What are you doing here?"

Ginger glanced at her mom, who kept smoking. "Didn't you tell him what happened?"

Glen sobered up quick. "What? What happened?"

"I left three messages on your phone." Their mom shook her head and walked out of the room.

Her brother narrowed his gaze on her. He resembled their mom with tight features and brown hair instead of red. "What's with her?"

"Dad's in the hospital. He had a mild heart attack and might need surgery. We'll know more tomorrow."

"Oh. Okay." Glen poured himself a glass of water, drank it down in one gulp then burped. "I'm going to bed."

Nice. Her brother showed his usual deep concern, but Ginger nodded instead of scolding him. She was over it. No more pointing out that he still lived at home and blew his weekly salary on weekend parties. Peter Pan had nothing on her little brother. But if he wanted to run with the lost boys the rest of his life, there wasn't much she could do about it.

Her mom must have also gone to her room because the house had quieted down. Growing up in the small three-bedroom ranch, heated mainly by the huge woodstove in the living room, Ginger had been surrounded by smoke and bad words. Settlers, all of them, never reaching out for something more.

How was she any different? So afraid to let go of what she knew. Too afraid to take a risk. Afraid of quitting one more thing because it might be hard to do.

She sat at the kitchen table and hung her head. "Please, Lord…"

She didn't have better words to pray. So many thoughts ran through her head and anger blistered her soul. She hated coming home. Nothing ever changed. She was supposed to be a light to their world, but had failed miserably. Over and over, she let them get the better of her.

She hated the snippy sound that leaked into her voice every time she came home. She hated to hear about how uppity she'd become living in Maple Springs. Ginger wanted to knock their heads together and yell wake up!

But what good would that do? What good could *she* really do? It wasn't easy digging for confidence when she felt like a failure in so many ways, especially around her family. Unless God wooed the heart, that organ remained stone cold.

She quieted her mind and asked God for strength and direction. Resting her head on her hands, she listened hard but heard nothing.

Then she closed her eyes and pictured Zach and his heart filled with icicles. The kiss they'd shared hadn't been cold or numb. It had felt warm and sweet. And right.

Envisioning that crooked half smile of Zach's made her heart pinch tight. What she wouldn't give to feel his strong arms around her right now, promising her everything would be okay. That he'd never quit when it came to the two of them. That she'd always be appreciated. She wanted to feel special and…loved. Maybe someday, she'd risk enough to trust Zach with her failures.

And even her dreams.

"Wake up."

Ginger jerked up with a start. Her neck hurt and her whole body felt stiff.

Glen laughed at her. "You've got a crease across your face."

She stuck out her tongue and then rubbed her eyes. "Where's Mom?"

"Getting ready. Did you sleep out here all night?"

"Good deduction, Sherlock." Ginger stood

and stretched, and immediately regretted her tone. "I'm sorry."

Her brother showed he cared by pulling her into a headlock. It was his way of hugging. "You okay?"

"Yeah." She pinched his underarm to make him let go. "I'm going to shower. Are you coming with us?"

Her brother rubbed his armpit. "Yeah."

And Ginger steeled herself for the family reunion about to take place in her father's hospital room. "Great."

"Don't worry, I got your back," her brother said.

And Ginger froze. Zach had once told her the same thing. A man of action, not flattery and words.

She challenged her brother. "Yeah?"

Glen looked away and laughed. "Nah, probably not. I'm driving, so you take Mom in your car."

"Thanks." That meant he wasn't staying.

As soon as things got hairy or vocal, he'd split. It's what Glen did. How was she any better? She'd moved away.

Two hours later, her brother did exactly that. Ginger looked over the insurance paperwork stacked in her lap and groaned. Could it be more complicated? Her father might be a bitter man, but right about now, he looked scared. He faced bypass surgery in the morning and there wasn't a thing he could do about it. No matter how much he ranted like a madman or swore at the nurses, he was going under the knife.

"You still got that store?"

"The Spice of Life?" Ginger sipped a cup of horrible hot chocolate, made a face and then tossed it. "Yep, it's open."

Her mother had gone outside for a smoke break, leaving her to deal with her father's nasty mood alone.

He shook his head.

And Ginger's hackles went up like always. "What?"

"Ain't going to survive."

Surly from a bad night's sleep followed by a worse day, Ginger let her temper fly. "What do you know about it?"

"Economy's no better, so who's going to spend money on fancy tea?"

Who indeed? The past few years everyone felt the lack of downstate tourists coming up north to take vacations and spend their money. But that was turning around. Last summer had shown promise. This summer might be even better. If she won the contest, that statewide advertising would give her store exposure. Make it a destination for those already vacationing up north. Maybe even online sales would increase. And that would make a difference.

"See, you got no answer for that one."

He knew more than she gave him credit for, but that didn't mean she'd agree. "Things are improving."

Her father snorted. "Pipe dreams. You're not getting any younger."

"What's that supposed to mean?"

"You fold up shop, what are you going to do then? Who's going to hire you with no degree?"

What is your time worth...

Zach wanted to hire her. But then what guarantees did she have for the future? She knew the challenges of running a business, especially one that depended on the fickle spending habits of tourists and summer residents. What if he got fed up with the headaches—she shook her head. She'd help with that, too.

"I'm not closing my tea shop."

"Stubborn." Her father said it in an insulting tone, but in his eyes she saw something she'd never seen before. There was a split second of pride shining in those cross brown eyes the same color as hers. Even some approval.

Something shifted inside her.

Maybe the one good thing she'd inherited from her earthly father was that stubbornness. Her father hadn't quit truck driving. After all these years, despite the complaints, he'd stuck it out. Maybe he hadn't settled. Maybe he'd sacrificed. For her.

She looked at her dad, seeing him for the first time in a different light. "Maybe I'll learn to drive a truck."

Her father looked surprised and then threw back his head and laughed. Hard.

"What's so funny?" Her mother had returned.

Ginger laughed, too, until tears clouded her sight. "Nothing."

Her father actually smiled. No, he beamed. "You wouldn't understand, Mern."

For the first time in her life, Ginger actually agreed with her father. Merna wouldn't understand, because her mother had given up a long time ago. But her dad hadn't, and he didn't want her to, either.

Zach heard the slam of a door and knew Ginger was home. They'd talked on the phone after her father's surgery went well and a full recovery was assured. Zach had offered to watch her store so she could stay longer, but Ginger was already on her way back. And she'd sounded eager to come home.

But that slam didn't sound good...

The slider whooshed open and then her

quick, hard footsteps stopped. "Why did you change the windows?"

He quit messing with the leftover blown hearts he arranged in a basket and faced her. One look at the fire in her eyes and he knew she either didn't get the message or rejected what he'd tried to convey. Neither one sat well, so he stalled. "For the contest win."

"But—" Her pretty mouth opened and closed. "You said you didn't care about that contest. This is supposed to be my win."

"It will be."

"How so, if it's all your work, like it's all your store? That's what you want, isn't it? To take over my space."

Where'd she hear that? "Eventually, yes."

She looked roaring mad at his admission. "When were you going to tell me?"

Keeping his voice even, he said, "Eventually."

She glared at him, her hair a mass of red curls that looked as if they hadn't seen a brush in a day or two. Her face was scrubbed clean and void of makeup, and she still looked beautiful dressed in plain jeans and a sweatshirt. She even wore normal, clunky winter boots. "So that's why you want me to work for you."

He stepped toward her. "There's a host of reasons why I want to work with you."

She lifted her chin. "Name them."

He lifted his eyebrow. "I'll give you the main one. You're wasting your talent selling a product you're not passionate about."

She openly gaped at him. "What are you talking about? I love tea."

She drank it. She didn't grow it, she didn't even dry it or mix the flavors together. She bought someone else's passion and pawned it off at a hiked-up price. Even her teapots were leftover inspiration from someone else. That was no way to live.

"I saw the look in your eyes after making that vase. You're hooked and trust me, that's all it takes."

Her angry gaze narrowed. "You can't push me into this."

How was he doing that? He spread his hands in surrender. "I need an apprentice."

"This is about *my* future."

"It's about us and—"

She cut him off. "I can't just jump on a whim. I have a twelve-month lease—"

"You might be broke by then—"

"How do you know?" Her brown eyes flared hot and her voice rose.

"I saw the spreadsheets on your laptop—"

She huffed and puffed. "That's none of your business!"

"It is when you're paying me rent." Things

were spinning out of control fast, but he was at a loss to get things back on track.

"Fine. I'll look for another place, then." She took a step closer.

"Not when you're bound to me for the next ten months," Zach growled. He'd sue for breach of contract if it'd make a difference. If it'd make her stay. With him.

"That's right, and like it or not, you have to honor that lease." With hands on her hips, she yelled back but her eyes looked too bright and watery.

He reached for her. "Ginger—"

She slid away from his touch. "Don't play me, Zach. I'm not for sale."

That was a slap in the face. "I'm not your enemy."

"No?" She gestured toward the windows and sneered. "Then what's with the sneak attack?"

Now she pushed him. And all his buttons by questioning his integrity. "If you had half a brain, you'd figure it out!"

Her eyes widened and then narrowed into slits of fury. "Yeah, well, I didn't get *my* college degree, but I'm not stupid enough to fall for—"

"I'm done with this." He cut her off, before she cut him to the quick.

She sniffed. "Fine."

"Good."

Ginger turned and left, closing the slider hard and then throwing the lock behind her.

He clenched his hands into fists. He wasn't sure what he wanted more, to shake sense into her or kiss her senseless. It didn't matter. He knew how that sentence ended.

She wasn't stupid enough to fall for him.

He looked at the windows and knew they were good. Once he'd flipped the switch on the spotlights that lit the glass as if from within, he knew just how good a job he'd done. Drivers heading down Main had slowed their cars to have a peek, and even people walking by had stopped and stared.

Ginger would get her contest win. He'd let her break the lease agreement early, too, if that's what she wanted. Let her move and set up shop somewhere else if she was too stubborn to follow her heart.

Or accept his.

When he'd kissed Ginger, he'd experienced something special. No, something incredible, and he thought she had felt it, too. Their souls had twined into one, blending like those little teapots she had ordered. But moonlight and dancing had a way of mixing up emotions, and he was only just beginning to feel. Like a newborn colt on shaky legs, he might be trying to run before he could even walk.

Ginger had made herself perfectly clear. If she wasn't stupid enough to fall for him, he should be smart enough to let her go.

Chapter Thirteen

Maintaining her distance from Zach hadn't been that hard. He'd buried himself in hot work when he didn't have customers to wait on. She remembered that he met with someone from the VA on Wednesday evenings, and Thursday he went out, too, but she didn't know where. He didn't tell her. In fact, he barely talked to her other than inane pleasantries that were so not him.

By Friday, Ginger wanted to scream. Her father's behavior in the hospital made a lot more sense after the week she'd had. Winter tourists flooded Maple Springs because of the upcoming three-day weekend. And shoppers looking to spend flooded Zach's studio, keeping him busy most of the morning.

Many had said the windows had coaxed them inside. Some even wanted tea, but most were interested in the twisted glass hearts and icicles for sale like those hanging in the display. They wanted Zach's work.

Maintaining her distance hadn't been easy, either. She missed the way they'd been. Ginger had caught the harried look in Zach's eyes several times as he waited on customers. He'd fumbled with gift wrap and growled at a couple of smart-mouthed tourists, but she stood her ground and ignored those terrible tugs on her heart to help him.

She would have helped, had Zach only asked. But he didn't.

Their argument remained a silent wall neither one tried to cross over. So she stayed glued to her own shop with her nose deep in the finance program on her laptop. Looking over her shop's historic trends, her future seemed pretty bleak.

She glanced at Zach's window decorated with icy blue twisted hearts and clear glass icicles. It was beautiful but a chilly reminder of the season. And his cold heart. Why hadn't he told her his plans? She would have appreciated some kind of hint. But he hadn't said a word, not one. Not even when she'd given him February's rent.

After a group of customers left, she spotted Zach heading toward his window. Snow fell softly outside. The postcard-perfect kind of snow that made everything fresh and pretty. She could hear laughter every now and then as people passed. Kids threw a snowball or two and lovers held hands.

Maple Springs was the place for lovers…

Her throat threatened to close up and choke her.

Zach stared at that snow. What was he thinking? His shoulders looked even broader when he folded his arms. Those strong arms had held her tight when she slipped. They'd held her close when they danced and circled her waist when he scared the book-man away.

Her heart twisted till it broke. She'd let him in and he'd hurt her.

He turned and caught her gaze. His eyes were cold, giving nothing away. The man had iron control.

Ginger's stomach pitched when he walked toward her.

"I'm going to grab lunch. Do you want anything from across the street?"

Her throat tight, she managed a rough-sounding, "No, thank you."

He looked at her a moment longer then left, locking the front entrance to his studio and flipping a note that he'd be back in a few minutes.

He didn't ask her to watch his store anymore, but he didn't bother to close the slider, either.

Ginger stared at the small OPEN sign he'd hung up the day after their fight. With a marker, he'd written on the back of it that he'd return. Simple as that. He didn't need her to watch over his store. He didn't need her at all.

She hated that sign.

She also hated that her display had been stupid and silly. A colossal waste of time and money. Zach's money maybe, but her time. She should have pushed harder for ideas. Good ones were right here, under her nose.

How much is your time worth?

Based on last year's net income figures, her time wasn't worth very much. Not much at all.

Ginger hung her head in her hands.

"Hey. You okay?"

Ginger popped up at the sound of Annie's concerned voice. She hadn't heard her friend slip inside. "I'm fine."

"You don't look fine. What's wrong?"

Ginger swallowed around the lump of emotion clogging up her throat. She did not want to cry. She didn't want Zach to see how much he'd hurt her. She didn't want to give him that kind of power, but then Annie touched her hand and Ginger fell apart.

Sniveling, she blurted out, "Everything!"

"Oh?" Annie's eyes widened. "Come on in the back and I'll make tea."

"But the shop." Ginger sniffed as tears fell and her nose ran like a faucet. She searched for a tissue.

Annie handed her a travel pack from her dance pants pockets. "No one's in here and I'll cover if someone does come in."

"But your class." Ginger blew her nose.

Annie waved it away and ushered her toward a chair in back. "Matthew's with John so I left early for my Friday class. I have time. Now sit, and tell me what this is all about."

Ginger's eyes welled anew and that stupid lump of heartbreak threatened to cut off her air along with her words. She dissolved into a pitiful fit of sobbing.

"Hello?" a masculine voice called.

Ginger made a move, but Annie pushed her back down in the seat while the single-serving machine chugged out a cup of hot tea. "Sit tight."

Ginger rested her head on her folded arms and listened. Annie informed the man that Zach had stepped out but should be back within the hour. Then she heard Annie close the slider door with a whoosh and thud. Smart move.

"Here, drink this." Annie rubbed her back as if she were a small child.

Ginger rallied to take a sip. She laid her head back on her arms and closed her eyes as the hot chamomile tea took hold and calmed.

Annie went about making another cup. "This has to do with Zach, huh?"

"Yeah."

"What happened?"

Ginger's anger burned all over again. She gestured toward the shop. "That happened. Did you see the windows?"

Annie nodded. "Yeah, they're gorgeous."

"Hmmph."

"I take it you're not happy with them."

Ginger wiped her eyes with a clean tissue. "He did that behind my back. Not once did he give *me* any ideas. No, he said to dig deeper and then bam, he changes my window display right before the voting opens and it's too late to change it all back."

"Why would you want to?"

Ginger glared at her friend. "Because he's trying to take over my store. He wants my space."

Annie chuckled.

"Why are you laughing?" Ginger's voice sounded shrill, but really, didn't Annie see the betrayal here?

"That's not all he wants. Have you looked at those windows, Gin? I mean, really looked."

"I try not to." She slumped and sipped more tea.

She'd avoided a full outside view from the front. Even jogging she'd taken different routes so she wouldn't have to spy the full spread in all its glory. Staring at what she could see from inside was bad enough.

Those two windows were a sore reminder of how she'd failed. When a couple of teenagers had stopped and ogled the display in her window, she knew it'd be better for business if she left it alone. And she'd been right, only most of the new customers coming in were looking for glass. Not spices or tea.

And that really rubbed salt in her wound.

"There's a definite message there."

Ginger rolled her eyes.

"He's a guy, and they don't always do things the way we expect, but they mean well. Give him a chance."

"I expect honesty," Ginger grumbled.

"How did he lie to you?" Annie's expression looked doubtful.

She shrugged. "He could have told me his plans. Instead, I overheard it from his sisters in the bathroom."

"His sisters?"

"Monica was talking to Cat or Erin, I'm not sure which, the night of your wedding. Evidently, Zach told her that he wanted to expand into my shop if he could convince me to give it up."

"But you have a signed lease for a year. You told me so. He couldn't legally take over your store until that ended."

Unless she gave it up early, because she thought he cared. Because he'd swept her off her feet while dancing outside in February.

Ginger grabbed her hair and twisted it into a tight bun behind her head. "I know."

"So, what's really bothering you?"

Hearing Annie's calm logic made Ginger realize how petty she sounded. She shrugged. "I'm scared."

Annie patted her hand. "I know, but sometimes you have to take a risk and see where it goes. No risk, no gain."

"Or loss." Bottom line, Ginger wasn't ready to trust Zach with her future. But was clinging to a failing business any better? The Spice of Life was all hers, but it was draining her dry. Financially and creatively.

Annie's eyes grew serious. "Love is worth that risk, Ginger. Even when there's a loss."

Her eyes burned. "You're going to make me cry all over again."

Annie's eyes filled, too, and her voice was soft but steady. "Zach's a good man. Go outside and see the message he's trying to tell you."

Ginger nodded.

"I've got to run. Call me if you need me, okay?"

Again, she nodded, because Ginger couldn't really speak. She gave her friend a fierce hug and whispered a ragged, "Thank you."

"You're my best bud." Annie squeezed back. "And you did the same for me."

Ginger waved as Annie left. Then she grabbed her mug of tea and returned to her spot behind the counter and her laptop. She needed to figure out her next move. Maybe she could learn to drive a truck like her dad. That crazy notion appealed now more than ever. No matter how much sense Annie made, Ginger wanted to run. Run away.

But not outside for a look at the window display.

She'd been afraid to really look at Zach's handiwork, because it would require a response. She'd have to make a decision about trust. Ginger had given her heart to a man with the power to shatter it like dropped glass.

And he might do that. Eventually.

Or maybe not. She'd never know if she didn't reach out and try.

I've got your back.

He'd said it. And Zach didn't blow smoke. He didn't say things he didn't mean. He was trained to look out for his own. It was no wonder that he had nightmares, when he felt as if he'd failed his men. He'd never put her in harm's way to serve himself. She should know that. But could she step out in faith and believe he had her best interests at heart with this one?

After eating lunch at a very packed Bernelli's across the street, Zach returned. He flipped the OPEN sign back around and glanced at Ginger's side. The slider door was closed. That sent a pretty clear message.

One he was sick to death of.

He strode toward that glass divider ready to rattle the thing off its hinges if needed. But one touch of the handle and the door gave way. She hadn't locked it.

Ginger looked up and her eyes were red-rimmed and puffy. "Oh, you're back."

"I'm back." Zach stepped into her shop. He'd given her space the past couple of days, hoping she'd come to him. But knowing that she'd been crying was the last straw. "We need to talk."

Her eyes grew wide and watery, but she lifted her chin. "So, talk."

He wasn't good with words, but she'd forced him to use them. "I'm sorry you had to hear about my plans for this place from someone other than me."

Ginger's eyes dimmed and she shrugged.

He spread his arms wide. "I did those windows for you and you hate them. I don't know what you want from me."

Bells jingled from behind them, so Zach turned.

Three women entered his studio with intent purpose. They didn't wander. Instead they headed straight for his counter. Now wasn't the time for talking with Ginger.

Clenching his jaw, he followed after them. "Anything I can help you with?"

"Do you have what's in your window for sale?" one woman asked.

"I'd like those flames." Another pointed toward Ginger's window.

"I have baskets over here." Zach directed them to each item and glanced again at Ginger, but she'd slipped away. Maybe she'd stepped into her back room for a moment.

And maybe he'd gone about this the wrong way. Maybe he needed to tell her straight up how he felt. If she didn't feel the same, at least she'd know that his motives weren't slimy as she'd accused. Maybe Ginger needed him to open up and share his feelings.

And maybe, Zach needed that, too. Sharing hopes and fears smacked too much of showing weakness, and Zach didn't like to feel weak. But Ginger had brought him to his knees. Playing this game of who'd flinch first was no way to fight.

It was time for someone to surrender.

The bells over his door rang again as more tourists and shoppers piled into his studio. A couple of women wandered into Ginger's tea shop. She was back behind her counter, looking more composed.

"Oh, you're not the same store," one woman said.

"No." Ginger looked straight at him as she answered.

He stared back.

But she looked away.

"I need a gift for my mother," another woman said.

"Does she like tea?" Ginger's voice sounded flat. A far cry from her usual upbeat energy.

He hated that she'd cried over what had happened between them. Hated that they'd wasted days angry at each other. Tonight, that ended.

He'd do whatever it took to hammer it out. To win her back.

He scanned his small retail space that was filling up fast with more customers. Skiers and sled-heads had poured into Maple Springs for Valentine's Day coupled with Presidents' Day on Monday.

He'd never made a fuss about Valentine's Day before, but then there'd never been a reason to. Tonight there was, and Zach wasn't about to waste his opportunity.

He spotted Rob dressed in jeans and a plain down jacket as the guy limped forward. No one would take him for the average tourist. "Hey."

"Thought I'd come down and check the place out." Rob nodded. "Nice."

Zach extended his hand. "I know. So have you thought about it?"

Rob returned the handshake. "A glassblowing class for veterans might be cool."

Zach laughed. "It's hot work that will make you sweat. A good place to get lost for a while, too. Come on, I'll show you around."

"What about your customers?"

Zach scanned the store, excited that Rob had not only come to check out the store, but might take him up on his offer of a class. "They're fine. They can wait."

They'd been in Afghanistan at the same time,

and Rob was having issues adjusting to civilian life. Zach explained the process of working with glass and then leaned against the metal worktable. "I'm thinking Tuesday evenings for a couple hours or so. Does that work for you?"

Rob nodded, looking both relieved and interested. "It does, yeah. Tuesday night."

"Say seven." Zach nodded.

"I'll be here."

"Good."

There were more veterans in the area, but Rob was a start. Only God knew where it all might go from here, but Zach was committed to doing something, and willing to find out the rest as he went.

While a couple of shoppers lingered, Zach walked Rob to the door. Maybe his work with glass shouldn't be about forgetting as much as remembering. His men deserved to be remembered well. Zach needed to honor them instead of trying to shut it all out.

Just as he was done shutting Ginger out.

He checked his watch. Almost five. Plenty of time to shower and shave.

When his last shopper walked out, Zach locked his front door, took down the OPEN sign and closed up early. He glanced at Ginger, but she was busy talking with Brady, the chamber president. No doubt about the festivities scheduled for the following morning to reveal the window display winner.

Zach knew what he had to do, and his heart raced. Way different from the rush before a mission, but equally nerve-rattling. It was go time.

Ginger closed up shop and her spirits had never been lower. Zach was gone. Without a word, she'd heard him go out the back door a while ago. She couldn't say that she blamed him. He'd wanted to talk, and instead of honey, she'd served up a strong serving of vinegar. Her sharp tongue had gotten her nowhere yet again.

Switching off the lights, she glanced at her tea and spice store illuminated by the spotlights that Zach had installed. The ruby-red hearts in her window glowed. They complemented her café table set with the red earthenware cups and red blended-heart teapot. Zach hadn't messed with any of that.

Love is worth the risk, even when there's a loss.

Losing her business was nothing compared with losing a loved one. Annie had lost her husband and survived. She'd even found new love with Matthew. Ginger remembered that Annie had been scared, too, but in the end it hadn't stopped her and love had prevailed.

What stopped Ginger? Like it or not, Ginger had fallen for Zach. Taking a risk meant stepping out in faith and trusting him with not only her livelihood, but her heart. Why was that so hard to do?

Ginger ran up the stairs to her apartment and bundled into a warm jacket. Slipping her phone into the pocket, she made her way outside. The snow had stopped falling and people walked the streets murmuring softly or laughing outright in the glow from the overhead streetlights.

Looking toward the north end of Main, she saw that soft lights shone from Valentine's Day–decorated windows. Reds and pinks and even silver were common colors used right along with tiny white lights. Maple Springs looked perfect. Inviting and romantic.

Keeping her sight focused toward the snow-dusted giant pine tree in Center Park, Ginger took a deep breath and crossed the street. Heart pounding, she whispered a prayer for courage, turned around and looked for whatever message might be in Zach's window display.

"Oh." Her breath caught.

Both windows popped like nothing else in town. If they didn't win, there was something seriously wrong because the display was indeed gorgeous. No wonder people had flooded inside to check out Zach's studio. The man was a genius. The spotlights he'd installed made the glass glow from within, full of life and feeling. And his passion.

She focused her gaze on Zach's window first. Intent on reading it like a sentence, she started at the far left side where he'd hung twisted blue glass hearts mixed with icicles. But as she followed the display toward her own window, those hearts grew more rounded and took on a pinkish hue. The icicles seemingly melted as well until they morphed into what looked like flames that began at her shop window.

Zach's heart had not only melted, it was on fire.

For her.

Her eyes watered and her stomach flipped, making her head feel light and woozy. But she kept reading the window message. Hers echoed Zach's with twisted pink glass hearts that blossomed into fuller hot fuchsia hearts and then finally those plump ruby-red ones that she loved.

Her tears spilled over when she finally spotted the sculpture. She'd never have seen it from inside because her café table had been in the way. At the lower right corner of her shop window, Zach had placed a large glass rendering of two hearts twined into one. It mirrored all the colors of the glass creations above.

And it was beautiful.

It was them.

Two hearts had blended into one.

Why had she let so many days pass before coming out here? Ginger slumped onto the park bench and cried. Zach's distance had everything to do with the wrong message she'd given him. Would he forgive her?

Grabbing her phone from her pocket, Ginger called Zach's number.

"Hey."

The sound of his deep voice made her tremble. "Zach, I got your message and I owe you an apology."

"What message?"

She sniffed. "The one in the windows."

"Where are you?"

"Across the street."

"Stay put, I'm almost there."

Before she could say another word, Zach ended the call.

She let loose an impatient growl and glanced up one end of Main and then down the other. Where was he?

The faint rhythmic sound of tinkling bells grew louder. Ginger spotted the horse and carriage the chamber had hired for the weekend coming up a side street.

Clop, clop, clop.

As the horse and buggy drew closer, she realized the man seated in the back was Zach. He held up a huge florist bag and a heart-shaped shiny gold box.

She laughed out loud.

The carriage came to a stop in front of her, and the horse jerked his head, nodding once, twice, three times. Yes, this was real. Zach was real and she knew that he cared. A lot.

He left the bundles on the seat and climbed out. Walking toward her, he held out his hand. “Ride with me.”

She took his hand, smiling over the tears streaming down her cheeks.

Zach pulled her close. “Why are you crying?”

“Because I’m wrong and so happy to be wrong. I’m so sorry, Zach. I’m an idiot, will you forgive me?”

He wiped away a tear with his thumb. “If you’ll forgive me for not telling you sooner that I love you. That’s why I want us to work together. We can build something good, you and I.”

“I know.” She didn’t think he was talking only about the glass studio and stepped out in faith and bared her heart. “I love you, too.”

He kissed her quick and grabbed her hands. “Come on, we’ve only got this carriage for half an hour.”

He helped her climb up into the seat and tucked the red plaid wool blanket around them both. Then he nodded to the driver. "We're good."

Tommy something-or-other, the treasurer's brother, tipped his tall black hat and clicked the reins, but he smiled, too.

Clop, clop, clop. They were moving.

Forward.

And Ginger wasn't ever looking back again. She reached for the gold box. "What's this?"

"Chocolates." He nuzzled her ear.

Ginger giggled and caressed the floral bag. "And this?"

"Red roses. What else?"

It must have cost him a fortune. "Zach—"

He shushed her. "Happy Valentine's Day, Ginger."

"My best one ever," she whispered.

"And it's only just beginning."

Then Zach kissed her.

And she kissed him back without any fear of the future. In fact, she could hardly wait to see what tomorrow might bring.

Chapter Fourteen

The next morning, Zach held out his hand to Ginger. She wore those impractical high-heeled boots again, and he shook his head. “Ready?”

She took it and grinned. “I am.”

“We might not win, you know.”

“We will.” Her confidence was catching.

He pulled her close and kissed her quick then looped her arm through his. They had a two-block walk to the Maple Springs Inn and it was snowing enough to make the sidewalks sloppy. With Ginger in those heels, they wouldn’t win any races.

“I can drive,” he offered.

“By the time you find a place to park, we could be inside and seated.”

She was probably right. This was a big deal with a big turnout by the sounds of it. “All right, let’s go.”

As they ambled along Main Street, traffic was busy, and the small lot at the inn was indeed packed full when they walked past. They entered the restaurant portion of the inn and Brady headed straight for them.

"They're here." The chamber president beamed.

"Who's here?" Zach asked.

"Reps from the department of tourism," Ginger clarified. Her eyes sparkled, too. This is what she'd been hoping for from the beginning.

"And they brought the big cameras, Ginger. I think we're in. Finally in." Brady rubbed his hands together. "It's finally coming together."

Ginger looked at Zach and smiled. "It sure is."

Zach smiled back. She'd have her shot at advertising her tea shop if that's what she wanted. He hoped she'd dump The Spice of Life altogether, but they hadn't ironed that out yet.

They hung up their coats and then hit the buffet table for Danish, fruit and various muffins. Zach followed Ginger through the maze of tables covered with crisp white cotton. He spotted Monica and she patted two open seats at her table.

"Follow me." Zach cut to the left.

Ginger met him around the other side of several tables.

"Morning." Monica gawked when he pulled out a chair for Ginger. "Wow, Zach, look at you."

"What?"

"Nothing." His sister grinned when Ginger scooted her chair closer to his.

"Happy Valentine's Day." He gave his sister a cheeky grin in return.

Monica sputtered and rolled her eyes. "Yeah, right."

He grabbed the vase from the middle of the table and sniffed the single red rose it held, but there was no scent. Not like the heady fragrance of the bouquet he'd given Ginger. She'd buried her nose in those blooms and told him that they were the first roses she'd ever been given. They wouldn't be the last.

He passed the vase to his sister.

"Who are you?" Monica teased.

Zach only draped his arm around the back of Ginger's chair. What could he say? He was a man in love. And he'd figure out a way to prove it. Soon.

"It's starting." Ginger sat up straighter.

Zach downed his coffee while Brady thanked everyone for coming. He launched right into a speech about the importance of the business community coming together on a common goal. The window display contest.

Zach glanced at his sister, who scowled as she stared at the chamber president. Something was definitely wrong there. "What's with you?"

"I'm not a morning person." She folded her arms and sunk lower in her chair.

He chuckled as his sister sulked. He sensed there might be more than that going on and was about to ask, when he felt Ginger's hand grip his knee.

The room had quieted, too.

Brady stood behind the podium ready to announce the winner. He took his time pulling an official-looking envelope out of his pocket. He put on a pair of reading glasses and cleared his throat. "An outstanding job on the windows folks, but one display received a landslide of votes."

And Brady paused again. For effect.

Zach nearly laughed. This guy was really hamming it up. But one look at the anticipation on Ginger's face and he covered her hand with his own. They had this.

Surely, they had this.

"And the window display winner is… The Spice of Life! Ginger Carleton, come on up and say a few words about how you put that window together."

Applause rang across the room.

Ginger gave him a look of pure joy.

He gave her hand a quick squeeze before letting go and then watched her make her way to the front.

"You two are sickening," Monica whispered.

Zach chuckled. "Thanks."

Ginger took the microphone and smiled. She looked beautiful with her hair a mass of red curls. She wore a fuzzy red sweater over tan corduroys, making her look like a Valentine. His Valentine.

"Thank you, Brady, and thank you to everyone who cast a vote. I really appreciate this, but I can't take credit for the window. And I can't take the prize."

Zach shook his head. What was she doing?

Ginger paused and looked at him, still smiling. "Not when it belongs to the artist who not only created the display, but won my heart in the process. Zach, this is yours. It's *all* yours."

He heard sighs run rampant around the room before it erupted again into applause.

He stared at Ginger. She offered more than a year's worth of statewide advertising. She'd given him her shop, her future and, more important, her trust in that one statement.

Monica pushed at his shoulder. "Go up there, you dolt."

He glared at his sister, but then the crowd chanted his name. They wanted him up there, too.

And Ginger waited for him, the minx.

He made his way to the podium, not once taking his eyes off hers. Although he didn't question Ginger's sincerity, he suspected her public display of affection was all about business. Their business. And he'd do what he could to help the cause.

Without hesitation, he wrapped his arms around her trim waist and pulled her close. Looking deep into her wide eyes, he kissed her. Hard.

Hoots and whistles rang out from the audience behind them. Camera lights flashed and still, he kissed Ginger. He felt her attempts to push him away slacken and then her hands crept up to hook around his neck. And she kissed him right back.

He finally broke away before things got out of hand.

Ginger swayed a little, bringing the crowd to laughter.

And Zach grinned, too, as Ginger's face blazed.

He took the mic from her fingers before she dropped it and addressed the crowd. "Thank you for the warm welcome back home." He raised the envelope. "This will come in handy for the studio as I anticipate a merger very soon." Then he looked at Ginger. "If she agrees."

The applause rose to a deafening volume.

And Ginger's mouth dropped open.

He was tempted to kiss her again, but gently tugged on her hand instead, guiding the way back to their seats. They were interrupted with congratulatory handshakes and pats on the back as they wove through the crowded tables.

He realized this was what he'd been longing for. Zach had not only come home, he'd finally found peace. And love.

"Why did you do that?" Ginger whispered close to Zach's ear when they finally sat back down.

He gave her that half smile of his. "Good for business."

The room had quieted while Brady talked about the importance of the contest and what made Maple Springs the perfect romantic getaway. But Ginger barely listened. She could hardly sit still, either. She wanted to know if Zach was serious.

What exactly did he mean by *merger*? "Zach—"

"I meant what I said."

Her heart rate picked up speed. "Yeah?"

He took her hand and leaned close, keeping

his voice low. "Be my partner, Ginger. At the studio and in my life. Be mine. Forever."

She blinked rapidly, fighting the tears that welled in her eyes. Love *was* worth the risk. They both had baggage, but together they'd work toward emptying those bags. Together they'd work to build something good.

With glass and in life.

Looking into Zach's warm blue eyes, Ginger had no doubts, nor fear. This wasn't quitting, this was one big, fat promotion. "Yes."

He brought the back of her hand to his lips for a swift kiss.

And then she gave him a wicked grin. "But I want it in writing."

He leaned close. "It's called a marriage certificate, sweetheart."

Ginger tipped her head and smiled. "Then I look forward to receiving that very soon."

He laughed.

The meeting ended and people swarmed their table. The state tourism folks wanted an interview, and Ginger overheard Monica on her phone.

"Mom, Zach just made a very public proposal..."

Ginger looked at Zach with pride. This man who'd grumbled over a hometown parade had just created a statewide buzz. It'd be good for business, sure, but watching Zach field questions with relaxed charm, she realized her future was in very capable hands.

Epilogue

"Zach, we made the spring issue!" Ginger charged through the back entrance, into the studio. She was back from a morning chamber of commerce meeting, where Brady had been proud to present her with a couple of copies of the state's tourism guide before he displayed them.

"Yeah?" He emptied the annealing oven of the glass flowers made the night before, along with globes and small birds made by Zach, Rob and another guy during class.

She didn't attend those workshops, but the flowers had been her idea. Zach liked a lot of her ideas, including a fall wedding so they could easily close up shop and run away for a two-week honeymoon.

She laid the magazine on the metal worktable and opened it to their article complete with pictures. There were shots of their windows along with that kiss at the podium. They'd been given the mock-up proofs ahead of time, but the real thing was even better.

As she smoothed the pages, her ruby engagement ring surrounded by smaller diamonds sparkled in the overhead light, and she sighed. "I love this ring."

Zach gave her a quick kiss. "Brady must be happy that Maple Springs made the cut."

"Ecstatic. Thanks to you."

"Us," he corrected.

"I like us." Ginger snuggled against him.

She meant it. They'd been busy remaking their two shops into one. She still sold loose tea leaves but only a few varieties for her repeat customers and Annie. She kept her big glass jars behind the newly updated counter and gift wrapping station.

That counter had a clear view into her old space that she and Zach had filled with new glass items they'd made together. All the profits from those things made by Zach's class went to a local fund for returning war vets.

Zach had even renamed the studio to reflect their business partnership. Z&G Glassworks had been etched into the center of both windows, and Ginger had to admit it looked classier than a sign. Especially with the way

Zach had designed the *Z* and *G* to look like two hearts twisted together. Blended into one.

Ginger no longer counted success in terms of what she accomplished alone. She had love and acceptance, and that made every hour of her day worth more than gold.

* * * * *

Dear Reader,

Thank you for picking up a copy of *A Soldier's Valentine*. I hope you enjoyed Zach and Ginger's story, the second book in my new Maple Springs series.

When first introduced in *Falling for the Mom-to-Be*, I knew Ginger would be the heroine of the next book. I loved her upbeat, tell-it-like-it-is personality and her thing with high heels! I can't wear anything higher than an inch, but I admire women who can.

Getting to know Ginger, I discovered that she struggled with her self-worth. Would she ever be good enough? I think we women battle many false images and beliefs about ourselves. And Ginger said something key—our minds can be a battlefield. Don't let the enemy advance. Instead, let's take back that ground by strapping on the Armor of God. Only through Him and His word can we see ourselves as we really are. Unique and precious in His sight.

I love to hear from readers. Please visit my website and drop me a note at www.jennamindel.com.

Many Blessings to you,
Jenna Mindel